everyone you love will be eaten by wolves

Steve Wetherell

acknowledgments

To Melissa McArthur for making all this coherent.

To Renee Miller, Robert Brumm, Jonathon Yanez and Noah K. Sturdevant for the motivation and opportunities they gave me. They are all very cool and you should check out their books.

To Mikayla Wilson for encouraging this out-of-character collection. And for all her support, in fact.

To EM Kaplan for the free reality check.

With sincere apologies to Rachel.

To my children, whom I love very much.

And finally, to my parents, and grandparents, who were all much braver than me, I think.

note from the author

Some people think it's a little pretentious for an author to introduce and contextualize the stories in a short story collection. I am one of them.

I am also a hypocrite.

the torso farmer

Originally published in an anthology called *Terrible Cherubs*, "The Torso Farmer" was my first real attempt at publishing something that wasn't pure comedy. It's also a story based almost verbatim on a nightmare I had. The subconscious isn't a reliable muse, but it throws you a doozy now and then.

People who read this story sometimes ask if I have considered becoming vegan, probably assuming that my acknowledgment of the existential horror of the food chain might curtail my base and monstrous appetites. Dear reader, it does not.

the torso farmer

IF YOU WANTED an easy life in Reclamation, you didn't let the bodies pile up. Dyson knew this from experience. If you kept the bodies shifting along nicely, then the fall from the conveyor belt in the ceiling almost always killed them. After all, they had no arms or legs to break their fall, so a snapped neck or a burst skull was practically assured. This being the case, it was an easy enough thing to spot the "A" or "B" branded on their chest, lodge the pitching fork under their chin, and heave them into the relevant chute.

It was when the bodies started to pile up that things got a little messy. If it was a busy day, or you were a little slow because maybe your back hurt, or maybe you were feeling a little demotivated because your wage allowance had gone down again, or your seventy-hour week had suddenly become an eighty-hour week, or because the Helping Hands didn't like the look of you and had decided to break your shins, then the bodies would create something of a cushion in the landing zone, and the fall became less than lethal.

This wasn't the end of the world, as such, but the way the torsos twitched and struggled and wept and stared at you was off-putting to say the least. At least they couldn't scream—

their mouths were sewn up before even the mechanical process that separated them from their arms and legs, before even the examination and branding. But they would struggle, which was odd, because they really shouldn't have been aware of what was happening to them. They shouldn't have had any references to pain or panic. Any references at all really, vat grown as they were.

Dyson used to perform a small mercy for the strugglers, twisting his pitching fork in such a way that it would break their necks, or at the very least choke them to unconsciousness, but on particularly busy days, there was not even time for that, and he would have to hurl them, weeping and jerking, into the relevant chute. He wondered if they suffered more in the reject chute, there to be incinerated to ashes, or the reclamation chute, there to have their organs carefully and efficiently removed before being dumped in the wash tub, where chemicals would soften their flesh for easy removal. He doubted any of the bodies survived long enough to experience being flayed utterly to the bone, but the thought sometimes made Dyson wake in the night, wondering who was screaming, realizing, embarrassed, that it was only him.

Today the flow was steady, and so far, Dyson was on top of things. He was a good worker: dependable, stolid. Twenty years behind the fork will give a methodical man a certain state of mind. He will ignore the ache in his back, he will cease to wonder at the ticking of the clock, and he will put one foot in front of the other while his mind floats somewhere else in a kind of hibernation, waiting for the whistle that would signal his reprieve. Not for Dyson, the crutches of the other workers in Reclamation. Not for Dyson, the stims to keep the mind perky, or the licorice flavor-rubs to filter out the smell of bad cheese and disinfectant.

Dyson was strong. Dyson was efficient. Dyson hadn't had a conversation with another human being in five years.

He jabbed with his fork and heaved a wobbling meat-sack into chute A. Behind him came the reassuring smack of skull on floor. He wondered if he was proud of his job, and realized with dull alarm that even if he was, would he recognize it? Was pride something he would know instinctively? Something that would reignite the blackened matchstick days? Unlikely.

Dyson would never know the feel of pride, but he could at least feel useful. His job was a necessary one, of course. Since the Great Malaise, ages long before his birth, the vat-grown clones were the only viable source of protein in all of Valhalla. Without them, the masses would have to survive solely on the vending machine splodges of brown vegetable mass, white vegetable mass, orange vegetable mass, and on holiday occasions, yellow vegetable mass.

When Dyson had first taken the position jovially referred to as "Forker," he had tried to give up the meat-patties. This was a usual thing, apparently, for new forkers. He had nearly starved himself to death before eventually giving in and bringing a patty to his lips. The vegetable allowances were simply not enough to live on.

To be fair, most of the masses enjoyed the meat-patties well enough. Oh, they knew where they came from, but there was a difference between knowing and looking into the weeping, terrified eyes of an adolescent quadriplegic about to face utter annihilation.

Every few months the Guiding Light would announce further progress in reclaiming the animal genome sequences from human donors, and there would be some token excitement and chatter at the possibility of conjuring a pig, or a cow, or even a chicken from the common cellular ancestry found in humans. The aim being, eventually, that they might resurrect the long-extinct animals and make them once again into slaves.

Dyson had surmised long ago that these announcements were inherently misleading in their optimism. After all, didn't he shovel up the results? The twisted spindles of limbs and tortured flesh that were inevitably stamped with a "B"? The mutants who didn't even need the fall to kill them, their lives already ended by erupting digestive systems or some otherwise betrayal of flesh?

No. There would be no chickens or lambs or cows in fields for the masses to lord over. And even if there were, where would they roam? What would they eat? If there was not enough processed vegetable mass for the people, then what would you feed the livestock?

Dyson suspected, deep in his sleeping mind, that society was something like a snake eating its own tail. The animals were gone, lost ages past to the malaise that took not just the beasts of the air and field and sea, but a goodly portion of all that was arable. They would not come back, and even if they did, would they want to? Would it be any better to put a dumb animal on these conveyor belts, other than a dumb clone? Would their suffering be any less? Would they be any less significant?

These were ethical thoughts, and Dyson, who had shoveled away a million or more soulless meat-puppets to their doom, had put on a shelf his understanding of ethical.

The masses were harvested, their genetic material mixed and matched in a hurricane of sperm and blood and science. Then they were processed, re-birthed for fuel and food and replacement organs. Then they were eaten. Then they were harvested. So it went on. It was not ethical, it was simply a kind of monstrous masturbation. Fucking yourself on an epic, species-wide scale.

Dyson bent his back to his work, his black skin made gray in places with dust matted to sweat, his muscles shifting and sliding like cable, his heavy brow creased over a blank slate of a face.

He contemplated the week ahead. The work, mostly, of

course. Eating the same meal he always ate in his cubicle-sized apartment. The state-sanctioned video games and drama-vids until the eventual sleep, which he enjoyed most of all. The maybe trip to a bar, where he might drink synthesized coffee and think about talking to people, but never actually would. The mandatory visit to the Spank Bank, where he would enter a musky booth, stick his dick in a portal, and watch a randomly generated holo-vid of whatever was currently popular in porn while a machine sucked him off and swallowed his genetic material. This would, of course, be the highlight of his week. Then the work again, always, forever.

Dyson was shook free of contemplation as his pitching fork found a struggler. His arms began to move without thinking, taking the necessary steps to end the faux-life before him, but stopped as the inner him realized something his wandering mind had not.

The struggler was him.

Down to the shape of the skull. Down to the heavy brow. Down to the one eye green and one eye brown that other people might find alluring had he ever looked anyone in the eye. The struggler was him, not yet dead from shock or blood loss, alive enough to look directly up at him. And Dyson saw something he had not seen before in the struggler's eyes. Beneath the usual hot panic and cold despair, he saw something that should not have been there. He saw recognition.

He felt an awakening of himself in that moment, as though his soul had suddenly caught up with his body after a long chase. He thought to cry out, to roar his outrage, to weep like a child and bemoan this fresh new horror. He did none of these things. He picked up the struggler by the neck and hurled it into the relevant chute. And though his body shook, and his mind screamed, and his guts swirled, Dyson worked the rest of his shift without comment.

At shift-whistle Dyson hung up his pitching fork and made his way across the metal-grilled floor toward the awaiting elevator. He swiped out his omnicard, pulled aside the gate, and stood with the likewise silent men and women of D-shift, all of them identically attired in the state-provided gray overalls and boots. There was a squeal that begged for maintenance as the elevator began its slow and juddering ascent from the basement levels. Dyson watched the other floors as he passed. The cutting room, the stamping room, the quality control floor, marketing, then the usual ten minutes of blank solid metal as they passed the laboratory floors.

Eventually they reached topside, which, as with everything in Valhalla, was really just a different basement. He trudged down the corridor, steps clanging in time with fellow workers, each of them filtering off into different corridors, their way lit by flickering track lighting. Those who lived in Valhalla made do with a little less than those who lived above them in Shangri La, who, in turn, made do with less than those above them in Nirvana. Dyson did not suspect it was a matter of class—they were all workers of one kind or another—it was just that the cleaners, maintenance men, and council-workers were all based in the upper floors, and so by the time they reached Valhalla, they had usually run low on an already stringent supply of fucks to give. Dyson supposed that this was just human nature, and that if he ever killed himself, he'd be sure to do it on an upper floor, so that his body might be found before it had turned to cheese-paste.

Even the ad-boards didn't work properly in Valhalla. Where the corridors in other levels rarely went a square foot without a neon billboard for this or that stim or sex-service, many in Valhalla had darkened, either fallen to vandalism or neglect. Dyson considered this a small blessing.

He trudged along, and when he passed a glowering contingent of Helping Hands, each a different shade of black in their poorly fitted plastic armor, he kept his gaze to the floor. Dyson was a big guy, and people liked to pick fights with big guys, especially if they knew that said big guy would not fight back. The Helping Hands said nothing at first, though one spat at his feet as he passed. Dyson walked on without comment.

"Why you looking at your shoes, clone-fucker?" called a voice behind him. "Don't you know you can't fuck your shoes? Why would you fuck your shoes, you clone-fucking mother-fucker?"

Dyson kept walking, resisting the urge to shake his head. He considered himself to be fairly dumb, but the Helping Hands would always make him feel like an unsung genius whenever they opened their mouths. He supposed that creative thinking was not a prerequisite to recruitment. Not that he'd ever suggest so. The Helping Hands were given relative autonomy in keeping order, and were enthusiastic in doing so. They might think you drunk and disorderly, or loitering with intent, or looking at them funny, and then they would enjoy breaking out every single one of your teeth with a billy-club before hauling you to a holding cell.

The holding cells were up near The Right Hand of Allah, and were supposedly each of them bigger than Dyson's apartment. He guessed there might be an irony in this, but he was not interested enough to dig for it.

Dyson rounded a corner and started as he almost bumped into a figure. A pasty white face with x's for eyes looked up at him from under a tatty beret. The figure stepped back, revealed as maybe a girl or maybe a woman—difficult to tell under the makeup, even if she was dressed in a manner to showcase as much of her skinny frame as possible. She didn't so much wear as ride a black mini skirt. A striped black and white top floated above her midriff, thin black braces pushed against clementine breasts. Her thighs were bare until the knee, when cheap stockings took over until the whole ensemble ended abruptly at a pair of ridiculously large red shoes. She grinned broadly with red lips and yellow teeth, put a gloved hand behind her back, and produced a bladder horn, which she honked at the same time as her other hand squeezed her breast. She gave a salacious wink that may have been text-book, if such a textbook existed.

Dyson blinked, puzzled, so abruptly pulled into human contact that he struggled to remember how human contact was supposed to go. The mime clearly wasn't a street enter-tainer, because street entertainers in Valhalla were rare as saints. More likely she was a sex-worker, the last bastion of entrepreneurialism in a world of government-rationed sex, drugs, and rock n' roll. Up against the state-sanctioned mega-whores and digital sex booths, common street walkers were constantly adapting to more and more specific kinks to stay in business. Dyson supposed that clown-fucking was among the least harmful of these.

"Sorry," he mumbled, but the words came out as bone-dust. He squeezed past and continued walking. The mime followed in step, matching his gait, wearing a comic expression of misery. Dyson turned to look at her and tried to remember how smiling was supposed to go.

The mime's eyes suddenly widened. She put a hand to her mouth as though shocked, and with her other hand lifted up the front of her skirt. There revealed a perfectly pale pussy, the jet-black pubic hair shaved carefully into an exclamation mark.

Dyson cleared his throat, making room for unfamiliar words. "I don't have any money," he said.

The mime sighed, then put two fingers to her lips, eyebrows raising in quiet question.

Dyson shook his head. "No, no vaporettes either. No stims, no pills, nothing like that. Sorry."

The mime bowed her head, looked at him with all the sadness in the world, and slowly rubbed her gloved hand across her belly.

Dyson sighed. Then fumbled in his overall pocket until he pulled out a half-eaten mash bar. The wrapper advertised it as chocolate flavor, its manufacturers knowing full well that nobody remembered what chocolate actually tasted like. "Here," he said.

The mime took it with a smile, and then raised her eyebrows in question again. She put a fist to the side of her mouth and stuck her tongue into her cheek. Dyson was a little while understanding the pantomime.

"Oh. Thank you, no. No, I have to get home. You have a good evening."

The mime shrugged, took a bite of the mash bar, and skipped away down the corridor.

"Don't go back that way!" Dyson called after her, his voice cracking with unfamiliar exertion. "There's Helping Hands back there. Looking bored, you know?"

The mime nodded, threw him a smart salute, and then marched primly in the opposite direction.

Dyson watched as she disappeared around a corner, then he watched the space where she had been for a while. Then he turned and walked on, alone.

Dyson was aware firstly of the ghost-lights wafting over his head, bulging and blurring from the bottom of his vision to the top before disappearing. Brief and complete darkness before the next light came and went. He was next aware that it was not the lights that were moving but him. He tried to open his mouth to comment on this, but could not. There was something keeping his mouth closed. He tried to reach for it, but could not. He had no arms. The lights came and went, and finally he became aware of the cold metal of the conveyor belt on his naked back. The scream in his throat was animal.

Dyson awoke, eyes wet, mouth dry. The thin, luminous strip above his door was the only light. He sat up in the dark and reached out for the faucet at the foot of his bed, using precious water ration in order to feel something real against his face. He was awake, and glad of it. The strip was blue, which meant it was some way 'til morning, but Dyson was in no hurry to return to sleep. He stood up, ducking slightly against the low ceiling of his apartment, and felt around for his work clothes. He patted his pocket to make sure the omnicard was still where he had left it, then he left his tiny room and returned to the empty corridors. He walked purposefully until he came to a bar where the signage had long since been lost to vandalism and apathy. It was mostly empty, though night shift was soon to end.

Dyson looked around at the darkened booths, some of them vacant, some of them haunted, before settling onto a stool at the bar. The barmaid had a face that time and circumstance had tempered into a permanent scowl. With a voice that couldn't care less, she asked him what he wanted.

"Whisky."

She raised an eyebrow. "I'm gonna have to scan your card first, buddy."

Dyson handed over his omnicard without comment. The barmaid scanned it on her console, her face briefly morphing with surprise as she saw the available credit.

"Ship come in, buddy?"

Dyson thought about telling the lady that he rarely spent what he earned, and briefly imagined a conversation wherein he orated whatever hidden philosophies he may have been hoarding for just such an occasion. It proved to be too daunting a possibility, and so he merely cleared his throat a little instead. The barmaid poured him his drink, setting it carefully before him along with his omnicard.

Dyson sipped at the whisky and was both shocked and elated at the unfamiliar burn. Alcohol was expensive, rarely bought when stims and synths were so much cheaper, but something in Dyson had decided that today was a day of import. He could not have told you why.

He sipped a tiny sip of his drink again and felt the itch of eyes upon him. He looked to his left where an old man was perched on a stool beside him. The old man grinned at him with fencepost teeth.

"Glad to meet ya, friend," he said. He spoke with a crow's voice, and he held out a hand that was all tendon and bone. "Glad to meet ya, glad to meet ya, glad to meet ya."

Dyson met the old man's gaze and saw the tell-tale signs of more drugs than druthers. He noted the white collar set into the black shirt. The old man saw him looking and straightened himself. "From God's lips to your ears, friend, sure enough. He tells me all I need to know, and I pass it 'round if I think a fella's worthy of passing on to. Do you think you're worthy, fella? Worthy of God?"

Dyson turned back to his drink and said nothing.

The old man snaked upright, his boney hand digging into the meat of Dyson's shoulder, his moldy breath in Dyson's ear. "Let me tell you, son, we think we left Him behind, but He's dug in deep to us. He's there all right, and He's waiting, and when we're finished finding the core of every sin, He'll be there with his balance sheet, friend, He'll be there with his balance sheet. Buy an old man a drink? Come on, rich boy, you buy an old man a drink and I'll save your fucking soul, buy an old man a drink and I'll pull you out of damnation, wouldn't you like that? To be pulled out of damnation? To feel the light of God upon your face again? You too good for the light of God, you shit?"

The claw tightened, the breath grew hot, Dyson stood suddenly and his own momentum knocked the old man back and off balance, where he sprawled against the bar stools. The old man looked up into Dyson's silent face and spoke through deep and awful tears.

"If we had any dignity, we'd starve. If we had any pride, we'd kill ourselves."

A voice rang out across the bar. "That's enough of that, you old bastard."

Dyson turned, flushed with guilt, and saw an agent of the Helping Hand stride across the floor with the confidence indicative of her position. She was short, young and freckled, forgoing the uniform black helmet to let her pink hair bubble out. Her hand hung at the holster of her baton as she walked over to the old man, who dropped to his knees before her.

"Oh holy God who sends His angels of darkness to punish me for my blasphemy, oh these terrible cherubs with their toddler minds and their monkey rage and their savage truths—"

The agent swung a kick at the old man's ribs, sending him into a coughing wheeze. "I said enough, you stupid old bastard. Ain't you got ears on your head? You fucking retarded? There ain't no sky man that listens to you, and if there was, he'd think you were a shit, same as me. You worship me if you need to worship something, you hear?"

She kicked the old man again, and then two more times for good measure, before turning to Dyson. "This old prick with you? He your daddy? He your boyfriend?"

Dyson shook his head, and the agent suddenly had a knife

in her hand, waving it over Dyson's face slowly so he could get a good look at it. It was an antique blade, a relic of a long-forgotten war, and if anyone else had held it, they would have found themselves in the cells without delay.

"You see that I'm serious, fucker?" the agent said. Her voice remained casual, and her lips, young as they were, stretched thin with self-satisfaction. "You see I'll take your face away if you fuck with me?"

Dyson nodded.

"You want to fight with your boyfriend, then you do it at home, you sick fuck. Understand?"

Dyson nodded.

The agent kept the knife at his throat but moved closer so that Dyson could feel the shell of her plastic body armor against his chest. His breath hitched as her fingers closed around his balls. She whispered in his ear.

"Or maybe I'll take something else? Maybe I'll take something else from you and feed it to your boyfriend there while you watch? Would you like that? Does that make you hot, you sick fuck?"

Dyson said nothing, stared straight ahead and dared not even swallow against the copper taste of fear in his mouth.

The knife was gone and the agent was walking away in a blink of an eye. She did not look back as she spoke. "Or maybe not? Who gives a shit?"

They stood there in tableau for a while: Dyson, the old man, the bartender. Dyson left his drink and went to work.

If you needed something bad enough then everything was too expensive. Valhalla always had a cheap fix ready somewhere, but for those far beyond cheap, the government-sanctioned highs were not enough. There were those suppliers and entrepreneurs who filled the gaps, growing, distilling and cooking up poison that even rats would turn their noses up at, had there been any more rats. The junkies, those who had quietly decided to die doing what they loved, came to those crooked cooks just as surely as a child to its mother.

Dyson's sister, Beko, had been such a child. Barely seventeen and already bent in ways beyond imagining. Mouth full of ugly tastes, head full of angry ghosts. So committed to her own destruction she'd surprised even the people fucking her with just how fucked she was.

She'd come back to her and Dyson's shared one room at a little past midnight, her skull filled with scavenged powders, her once brilliant black skin faded to the gray-blue of a bloated tick. She had woken up her younger brother and talked to him at length about spirals while the slow trickle of blood from her nostril became a gush. Then she had died, leaving Dyson alone and just twelve.

Eventually they'd heard him crying and sent the Helping Hands to take the body, without telling him where to—a small and surprising mercy.

One of the suits had come to see him, a rounded man with rounded glasses and a ridiculous tie. He'd explained to Dyson that, although he no longer had a big sister to take care of him, he would have the next best thing: a job so that he might take care of himself.

And so Dyson, small, stupid and weak, went to work.

In time he became a man. Whatever that was.

Dyson clocked on to D floor far earlier than usual. The first thing he saw was the mountain of bodies. A slip-sliding pyramid of wrecked flesh in beigey-brown hues, slick with rivulets of red. A totem of obscenity. A thing of things.

With every other heartbeat, a new torso wheeled in from the conveyor belt in the ceiling, flumped onto the pile beneath it, rolled and gaggled like a silly game. Came to rest, struggling, bleeding, merging. There was the background gurgle of many throats trying to scream through sealed lips. There was the feel of a thousand glaring eyes, not all of them dead.

Dyson stood before the pyramid in revered silence, an acolyte before a strange new God.

The night-shift worker, maybe ten years younger than Dyson and boney at the shoulders, stood with his pitching fork dangling in his hand. He turned around and revealed a face raw from tears, shiny with terror.

"I just kinda thought—what if I just stopped, ya know? What if I just stopped doing it?"

He pointed at the pile with a shaking hand, his pitching fork dropping to the floor with a clatter.

"Nothing happened. It didn't stop. It just goes on." The lad's lips began to quiver. "It doesn't stop. Oh, Jesus what do we do, man? What do we do?"

Dyson slowly bent and retrieved the pitching fork. He pressed it into the younger man's hands. "We dig, son. We dig."

The boy and man worked, harder than either ever had. Dyson felt fire blossom in his back and his knees and his shoulders, but there was fire elsewhere too. Stomach. Heart. Head.

When the boy faltered, fumbled, and eventually fell, Dyson dragged him clear and began to dig again. Bodies were heaved and thrown, making hollow clangs against the metal sides of the chutes as they tumbled away into darkness.

He worked. Oh, how he worked.

Dyson's head eventually tuned out from his body, until the rasping of his breath and the thudding of his heart became hymns in a distant cathedral of agony. He saw face after face before him, women, men, young and old, clones and the processed dead alike. Mutants, failures, food and sustenance.

Once he saw his sister's face, gray and scabby at the nose, beseeching him through sewn-up lips for one more fix. Once he saw a body still bearing smudges of white makeup, its pubis adorned with mad punctuation, its sex made a punchline. He saw a priest. He saw a bartender. He saw his own face again, many times, sometimes as a boy and sometimes a man (whatever that was).

Most of all he saw the fork and the chute and nothing in between.

He had become an engine of sheared gears and red-hot bearings by the time relief finally tapped him on the shoulder. The woman who took over his shift frowned at him, perhaps seeing that Dyson was only slightly there, a ghost haunting his own body.

"You okay, chief?"

Dyson said nothing, his tongue dried to the roof of his mouth, his throat closed to a tiny hole. He breathed open-mouthed, a guppy in a desert.

The woman nodded to the slush of bodies beneath the chute. "You on a go slow or something?"

Dyson stared at her a while, and then grinned, face stretching in unfamiliar ways. Over the permasound of moving parts and buzzing wire, he laughed until he thought he might die.

The elevator door opened, but only with protest. Dyson, placing one foot in front of the other as a toddler might line up bricks, stumbled in and fell heavily against the wall. Those other workers, clocking off, clocking on, paid him little heed.

Dyson listened through ringing ears to the people talking.

"They say I'm transferring to the bikes next week, but I'll believe it when I see it. Ain't that the life? Get to sit, at least, huh? I did a few months on the treadmills, but it ain't the same. Slow down on those things and you say hello to all the feet behind you. We used to fight to get to the front where the handle was, or else stay at the back where all you had to worry about was dodging the odd clumsy asshole. You could make a game of it.

Most of them survived it, you know, just got up and got back on again. Some didn't, maybe if they got stepped on too much. Used to be a couple of Helping Hands stood by, just pick 'em up and chuck 'em in the reclamation chute. You know, some of those guys, I know this, man, I know this. Some of those guys weren't even dead. Just dog tired. Same thing to those fuckers, though, right? Damn right.

The bikes, though? Sweet deal if you've got the knees for it.

Dyson slowly slid down the wall, cheeks cold and throat dry. Darkness took him down through the metal grilled floor and on to somewhere silent.

The elevator door opened. The light was like none he had seen before. Dyson got to his feet and, crooked and wincing, stepped out of the elevator.

There was green, green like he had only ever seen on vid screens. There was grass, softer than his mattress. There were trees that were pretty, nameless and laden with…fruit, probably. He looked behind him to see that the elevator was housed in a gleaming metal box, the only manmade object in a field of improbable nature.

Above Dyson was sky, and the sight of it nearly pinned him to the ground. Stars. An impossible multitude of stars.

More than all the bulbs in Valhalla, surely. As he watched, there was a faint violet shimmer that rippled across the sky.

"A vid screen?" he murmured.

"No, not that, my friend. The stars are real enough, just behind a pulsefield is all."

Dyson looked to the man who had approached him. A familiar voice. A familiar face. Both his own.

"Welcome, friend."

The man who was not Dyson smiled in a way that Dyson had never smiled. The one eye green and one eye brown nestled comfortably in cheerful creases. The teeth bared easily and prettily. The man was dressed not in overalls, but in a loose gray shawl and baggy trousers.

"What is this?" said Dyson. "What floor am I on?"

"The top floor... Dyson, is it?" The man held Dyson's omnicard in his hand, peering down at it. "Though I'm a little puzzled as to how you got here. You're not authorized to be on this floor."

"The top floor?" Dyson mouthed the words as though tasting a foreign tongue. "I...don't know." He gestured around him to the floors of grass, the walls of trees, the ceiling of stars. "What is this place? Who are you? Are you the Guiding Light?"

The man who was not Dyson smiled again. "More like the people who guide the Guiding Light."

There was a movement and another figure approached, seeming to appear from very far away and coming closer faster than her languid pace should have propelled her. She too was dressed in loose, gray clothes, and under the thatch of silver hair, Dyson thought he saw a familiar face.

"Do I know you?"

The woman looked at Dyson with barely concealed bemusement. "I should think not." She turned to the man who was not Dyson, kissed him slowly on the mouth. "This your boyfriend?" she whispered. The man laughed.

The woman turned away and as she did, plucked one of the strange fruits from a low hanging branch. She tossed it to Dyson, who caught it awkwardly.

"You look hungry," she said, and then turned and walked away, her body traveling far further than her steps should have taken her.

The man nodded encouragingly at Dyson. "Go ahead."

Dyson bit into the fruit, juice slapping his chin. He did not have a word for how it tasted.

"Good?" said the not-Dyson.

Dyson nodded.

"Why are you here, Dyson?"

Nothing.

"Shall I tell you why you're here?"

Less.

"You're here because the world gave up. We fucked it so hard it just gave up, then we fucked it some more. Fucked it 'til it stopped twitching. And when it did, when the Great Malaise took hold, we left. Those of us who could. Those rich and clever and pretty. To find a new world to fuck."

Dyson looked up at the ceiling of stars, realized that they were moving, slowly.

"But captains need a crew. This journey will take many lifetimes, you see. So who do we hate enough to man the bilges and stoke the boilers? Without beasts to burden, who do we hate enough to enslave for all of time?"

The man took Dyson's hand in his own. "We are not so awful a people that we don't recognize our need for redemption. Who do we hate enough to feed our machines and our bellies? Why, ourselves, of course. Each pioneer his own master, his own slave, his own sustenance. And ain't that just karmic?"

Dyson snatched back his hand, exhaustion breeding a strange form of defiance. "Is it? Then how come you're up here and I'm down there? And how many of us sweat to skeletons so that you might see the stars and walk on nature?"

The man smiled, palms open. "Do you prefer we all suffer in the dark? We are exactly the same, you and I, bar circumstance. If it were you up here and me down there, would it be any different?"

Dyson tried to spit through his dry mouth. "Might make a nice change."

The man shook his head. "Nothing would change. Not really. And besides, this isn't forever. We scrabble in the dark, but we move toward the light. A better world awaits us."

"Where? When?"

The man shrugged. "Fuck knows, hombre."

Dyson stepped back, dizzy and tired. He sat down on the floor. "Why me?"

The man knelt down, put his fingers to Dyson's cheek. "Why anybody? Why anything? Things are the way they are. You aren't being punished, Dyson. No more than any of us are. You didn't do anything wrong. Your only mistake was breathing in and out."

"Is that a fact?" Dyson mused. "Was that my mistake?" He felt gears slide inside himself, clockwork that had run dependably for his entire life seizing and jumping. "And is that your mistake? Is that your mistake too? Here, let me fix that for you."

Dyson stretched out his strong, rough hands, catching the man by the throat. He squeezed, watching the one eye blue and one eye brown bulge in the man's sockets, his face becoming a rubber mask.

"Is this your mistake?" Dyson screamed. "Is this my mistake?"

He tightened his grip, the face before him turned scarlet,

then maroon. The eyes popped obscenely, but the mouth smiled. Even as a swollen purple tongue erupted like puss from a zit, the mouth was smiling. As Dyson squeezed harder, his vision began to darken, his head began to lighten. For a moment he was nothing but a pair of grasping hands. Then he was nothing at all.

Dyson was aware firstly of the ghost-lights wafting over his head, bulging and blurring from the bottom of his vision to the top before disappearing. Brief and complete darkness before the next light came and went. He was next aware that it was not the lights that were moving but him. He tried to open his mouth to comment on this, but could not. There was something keeping his mouth closed. He tried to reach for it, but could not. He had no arms. The lights came and went, and finally he became aware of the cold metal of the conveyor belt on his naked back. The scream in his throat was animal.

If you wanted an easy life in Reclamation, you didn't let the bodies pile up.

the last reading of madam shahrazad

I almost always write fantasy. There's rarely a project I get enthused about that doesn't include magic or improbable science. This is because the real world is, frankly, boring and badly organized. As far as I'm concerned, the only purpose of the real world is to engender fantasy.

That being said, when Renee Miller of the Deviant Dolls asked for a contribution to an anthology, I thought I'd challenge myself to write something set in cold, hard reality. I had a lot of fun throwing away my familiar crutches, but my characters sure didn't. Turns out some people need a little magic in their lives...

the last reading of madam shahrazad

MADAME SHAHRAZAD WAS NOT her real name. Nor was she a descendent of Gypsy royalty. Nor could she speak with the dead.

Her real name was Stacey James, a name that cried out to sell real estate in one of Florida's ever-expanding gated communities that were packed with the retired, the comfortable, and the dying. But she did not sell houses.

She was not descended from Gypsies, but she thanked her Iranian grandmother for her foreign nose and dusky complexion. Had she been as white and conventional as her namesake, she doubted very much she could spin her false Romany heritage so convincingly. Many of her clients had never set foot outside of their identical residential blocks, but they had expectations. A little heavy on the eyeliner, a little red on the lipstick, and they never guessed that she was from exactly as far away as the next town over.

She did not speak with the dead, in her enriched anywhere-but-here accent. Well, she spoke *to* them, certainly, but they never spoke back. Obviously. They were dead. Madame Shahrazad, like all psychics, had exactly as much supernatural ability as a cat, or a toddler, or a gator. That is to say, none.

But Stacey made a very healthy living in convincing people that Madame Shahrazad did have supernatural powers. This was easier than it sounded because the people who sought out Madame Shahrazad already desperately wanted to believe that she could commune with spirits. Stacey understood what every con-artist, politician, and whore knew in their bones—that people mostly believed what they wanted to believe and would go to great lengths to fool themselves if it meant avoiding a harder truth.

This is not to say that Stacey was without talent. People gave her money, after all, and even the most wide-eyed true believer gets a tiny dose of reality whenever they open their purse. Stacey had talent. The clothes, the accent, the fake Gypsy heritage—those were all tools, subtle little hooks that let a client suspend their disbelief a little more securely. Stacey's real talent was cold reading, the careful mix of charisma and trickery that could lead a person into telling you exactly what you wanted to know, without them even realizing they were doing it.

Sometimes it was all terribly obvious. "I sense your grandmother led a full life." Well. Duh. "I sense your son was taken too soon and is greatly missed." Gasp. Really? But any fairground hack could pull that amateur shit. It took someone with a keen eye and a quick mind to make the kind of connections Stacey could make. Look at their jewelry, their makeup, their eyes, their clothes. Look at their body language, look at what they do with their hands. Stacey could slap together a profile of a person often within a few seconds of meeting them, and she was rarely wrong. Her intuition was so good, she didn't wonder that some people, dull people, attributed it to magic.

The rest of her act was finding out what people wanted to hear, and letting them hear it. No magic in that. You learned that growing up. Getting your friends to do your homework.

Getting guys to buy you drugs. Getting your mom to divorce your stepdad. Getting a couple of drunks to beat the shit out of your ex. Easy. Kindergarten stuff. The act was even easier because, when you got right down to it, everyone who came to Madame Shahrazad wanted to hear the same thing. They wanted to hear that everything was okay. And they wanted to believe it. They really did.

Right now, Stacey wanted to believe it too. She wanted to believe that the pulsing in her head was a hangover. That the strange room she was in belonged to some guy or girl she had picked up. She wanted a happy explanation for why her wrist was sending rips of agony through her arm. Why the seat of her thighs were wet and raw. Why she could taste cloth.

There was no reassuring explanation, though. Though she still wore her bed clothes—an old Sepultura t-shirt taken from a long-forgotten boyfriend—the room was not her bedroom. Not anyone's bedroom. It was too empty, with a dark and dusty concrete floor that rolled out into shadow. When she tried to call out and heard only a muffled groan, she knew the cloth taste was from a gag, probably a rag rolled up in her mouth. She could just about make out her left hand in the low light, enough to see that the wrist was swollen to a good three times its proper size. Enough to see that, much like her right hand, it was secured with cable-ties to the arm of a chair she was sat in. The chair that was still sticky with a puddle of her own piss, the smell of which was only adding to her rising nausea.

"You're awake."

The voice was flat, hard, and echoed back from un-seen walls. Stacey concentrated as much as she was able, and the figure before her came into focus. It was a man, a big guy, carrying more than his fair share of gut, which was not so unusual in Florida. He was broad at the shoulder and his brown leather jacket looked too small on him. His voice had been hard, but his face looked soft—chubby cheeks and a blond furze of beard lending him a patina of youth. The light, wherever the light was coming from, reflected in his round spectacles, turning his eyes to twin, alien moons.

"You're awake," he repeated.

Stacey couldn't remember the last time she had been truly afraid. She felt now that she might piss herself, had she not done so already. She noticed to the figure's right a collapsible camping table, but it was too dark to see what was on it. Her imagination supplied plenty of options, though, none of them reassuring.

There was a wet sound as the man before her swallowed. "Listen," he said. "Listen. I'm gonna take out your gag, okay? And I want you to think about that. I wouldn't take it out if I thought anyone was going to hear you scream, right? Nod if you get me."

Stacey nodded, but thought she might scream anyway. She was going to be tortured. Raped. Killed. You heard about it all the time. Some sick bird's well of darkness finally reaches its overflow, and he takes it out on the nearest pair of tits.

Some cynical part of Stacey's subconscious had already decided the best possible outcome.

Make it quick, make it quick, make it quick, please God I know you're not there but make it quick, make it quick.

She flinched and shuddered as the big man reached slowly toward her. As his fingers neared her face, she smelled a faint lick of lilac. Then suddenly the gag was out of her mouth. She heaved in huge breaths, whimpering on the exhale with a whine unlike any sound she had ever made before.

"Please," she said. "Please, don't, please."

"Shut up," said the man, calmly. "I need you to shut up."

"Please no, no, no, no—" Stacey was cut off as she felt a heavy hand cuff her face, and her world was briefly taken up entirely by her tingling cheek.

"You done?" the man said. "I don't want to have to do that shit. I mean, I will. You done?"

Stacey stared wide eyed up at him, and then nodded quickly even as she began to sob. She heard the man sigh and a loud scrape as another wooden chair was dragged before her. The man sat down and slouched like someone waiting to be called for a routine checkup.

Gradually Stacey's breathing began to slow. Eventually her jaw stopped shaking enough for her to speak. "Where am I?"

The man cleared his throat, his face impassive behind his weird, shining spectacles. "You're in an old garage. You don't need to know where. You just need to know that you're miles from another human being. Nobody comes here. Nobody drives by here. Ain't nobody going to hear you or come for you."

Stacey felt her shoulders begin to shake again as panic struggled inside her like a rabbit in a snare.

"Now stop that," the man said. "We don't got time for that. Ain't nothing gonna happen to you 'less you do as I say."

Stacey nodded and looked at her feet, trying to will herself to stop shaking. Did she believe him? That he might have his way—use her to scratch whatever deep and awful itch he had—and then turn her loose? Maybe if he'd hidden his face, she might think so. But even then, with what they can do with DNA, why would he risk letting her go? If you're not squeamish about kidnapping and raping a woman, it's a safe bet you'd be able to steel yourself enough to bash her skull in, or choke her out, or cut her—

"You listening to me?"

Stacey looked up, shaken from her inner snuff matinee, of which she was the recurring star.

"Calm down, don't get yourself worked up. My name is Pete."

Why would he tell her his name? He stared at her, seemingly waiting for a response. Stacey cleared her throat. "My name is—"

"I know what your name is." For the first time, the man's voice, Pete's voice, took on an edge of menace. "Stacey James. Or should I say Madame Shahrazad." Pete made a grandiose gesture as he said this, waving his arms like a cartoon wizard. "Yeah, I know what your name is."

Stacey had felt her heart jolt in her chest as he said her name. She didn't recognize the man, not at all, and she had an almost photographic memory when it came to faces. He knew her, but she most certainly did not know him.

"Here." Pete stood and went to the table, where Stacey could now see there was a leather bag, the kind of unremarkable bag you might put a laptop in.

Or a knife, or a hammer, or a pair of pliers, or—

"Here." Pete held out two white pills in his hand.

Stacey felt dread wash through her guts. She began to shake her head.

Pete sighed impatiently. "It ain't to drug you, okay? I don't... I don't need to do that, right? This is because of your wrist. Now, go on there, take 'em."

Stacey continued to shake her head, unable to stop the motion.

"Dang it," Pete said, and sat down in the chair again. "Look, here's what happened, okay? Don't freak yourself out, just listen. I was in your house last night. Came in while you were asleep. Put a rag with chloroform over your face. Like in the movies, you know?"

Shock, terror, and disgust fought for dominance in Stacey's brain. He had been in her house? Her room? She had a sudden flash of memory, perhaps real, perhaps imagined, of struggling to breathe and an awful chemical smell.

"That's your headache, there, I should imagine. Looked it up on Google." Pete made a wiggling typing motion with his fingers. "You probably have a pretty bad headache right about now. Your wrist, though, that was kinda my fault." He sucked in breath between his teeth. "I was putting you in the trunk of my car and I kind of, I kind of slammed the trunk on your hand there. I didn't mean to do that. I'm sorry about that."

Sorry? He was sorry? Stacey felt a spark of anger, a brief and welcome distraction from the terror. This man kidnaps her for God-only-knows what reason, and he apologizes for being clumsy about it?

"So, I got these pills," Pete continued. "My mom used to take 'em for her back." At that, Pete paused a while and stared into some private memory before shaking himself back to the here and now. "Anyway, they're real good. They'll take your mind off the pain in no time at all. You gonna take 'em, or do I have to hold your nose?"

Stacey dropped her mouth open obediently and tried not to shudder at that brief lilac smell as Pete placed the chalky tablets on her tongue. She tilted back her head and swallowed the pills dry.

"Here, I've got water." Pete went into his bag again and brought out a plastic bottle of Calusa Spring, waggling it like a treat for a dog. "You want some?"

Stacey didn't want to take anything from this man, nothing at all, but her throat was dry and her teeth felt like dirt in her mouth. Something inside her more persistent than caution took over, and she nodded her head and opened her mouth once more. Pete unscrewed the cap and brought the bottle gently to her lips. The water was cool, and she slurped it greedily until she could feel her stomach swell and hear the crunching sound as the plastic bottle imploded.

She sat for a while gasping her breath back. As much as it seemed a ludicrous comparison, given her situation, she actually felt better.

"Why?" she said.

"What?"

"Why am I here? What do you want with me?"

Pete didn't reply but went to his bag again. He came back and a flier landed in Stacey's lap. She could barely see the words, but she didn't need to. She knew the words by heart. After all, she had written them.

Madame Shahrazad
14th Generation Romany
Spiritual Medium & Advisor
"Let Me Bring You to Peace"
Book Your Consultation Now

The flier was understated, tasteful. She had found long ago that, in her line of work, a gentle whisper worked far better than a touter's shout. In fact, she barely used the fliers, relying much more on word of mouth and repeat business to keep her schedule full.

"I want you to do a reading." Pete grinned. "Is that what they call it, a reading?"

Stacey paused a moment. She recognized Pete's tone. You didn't get far in her business without running into cynics, and criticism mostly manifested in sneering and mocking, which she preferred much more to threats of legal action. She responded almost automatically, in the way she'd respond to any vocal critic, which was to Keep Calm and Keep in Character.

"I can consult cards, if that is what you mean. I cannot read your palm, though. That is a different art entirely, one not passed down to me by my—"

"What's it called when you talk to dead people? What do you call that?"

Stacey found some small comfort on familiar ground and made herself look up to meet Pete's eye. The man was leaned forward, and the reflected light on his glasses was gone. Up close his eyes were a pale blue, and he looked at her not with malice, she saw, but with a look she had learned to spot like a hawk learns to spot a mouse. A look of sadness, run through with hope.

"We call it communion. Communion with the spirits."

Pete nodded, slowly. "Well, that's it, Madame Shahrazad. That's what I want from you. I want to commune with the spirits."

Stacey held his gaze for a moment. Despite her fear and disorientation, old habits were kicking in. Stacey considered herself a professional. Hers was no part-time gig. She had given up on Stacey James ten years ago and had made her living, a very good living, as Madame Shahrazad ever since. At only thirty-five (a baby compared to most mediums) she had favorable mortgages on three small houses, two of which she rented out at a modest income. And she had ambition. She was good. Really good. Getting on public access talks shows or guest spotting on local radio might seem a little dream for most people, but Shahrazad was no slouch, and she had realistic ambitions. Local TV, self-published books, paranormal convention appearances, it all added up. Stacey James would have lived and died in a trailer park, failing away at some temp or waitress job, probably falling into some convenient relationship to split the bills. But Madame Shahrazad had plans. Madame Shahrazad was on the up and up, headed for an early retirement on the Florida Keys where she would live out her days banging too-young waiters and smoking good weed. And she'd do it. She'd achieve it. Because she was a professional.

She looked at Pete now, really looked at him. She carefully played back everything he had said to her. She took a long slow breath in through her nose and let it out. She would take a chance. Even as part of her screamed to stop and think about what she was doing. You didn't get to be Madame Shahrazad, rising star in make-believe bullshit, without being able to front it out when the pressure was on.

"Did you want to talk to your mother one last time?"

She could tell by Pete's body language that she had scored a direct hit. She kept her face impassive, but inside she was pumping her fist. She could take control of this. She could turn this around.

"I understand. I sense a great despair in you, and in times of great despair sometimes we do things that—"

"Shut up." Pete stood at the fold-out camper table, staring away into the shadows, the bulk of his shoulders rising and falling, slowly. "Just shut up and let me think."

Stacey nodded and kept quiet, watching the big man's shoulders rise and fall, rise and fall.

"Is this you now talking to dead folk?" he said. "Did they tell you about my mom?"

Stacey measured her next words carefully. "I hear the voice of a spirit guide, a familiar on the other side. He sees much, and can see—"

"So dead folks, right? You're doing it now. You can just talk to dead people, just like that?" Pete turned around, and Stacey was horrified to see that he had retrieved another item from his bag. A snub-nosed revolver, black and weighty with awful promise. "Just like picking up a phone?"

"Not exactly." Stacey swallowed. She was surprised by how suddenly calm she felt. The stakes were terrifying, the situation insane, but they were playing her game now. The paralyzing fear she had felt just minutes ago had all but left her. What was left was the game. "I need to concentrate, to meditate…"

"But you said just now that you were talking to a spirit

guide." Pete frowned in agitation and gestured carelessly with the revolver. "You did, you said just now!"

Stacey flinched as the barrel jabbed at her and spoke carefully through gritted teeth. "My guide is always with me, but the after world, the astral plane, is beyond measure. I need to concentrate, to call out, to become a beacon to those who are sought. If not, I'd be overwhelmed by uncountable voices. Don't you see? You mentioned picking up a phone, but that's not right. It's more like tuning in a radio, searching for a lost and very faint signal."

She looked up and found neither satisfaction nor annoyance in Pete's face. She knew a good lie wasn't something you just unfurl like a car in a show room, it was something you had to construct like a tower. Strong foundations now would be vital when it came to shakier truths down the line. She felt something like a fist unclenching inside her as Pete began to nod slowly.

"Okay," he said. "So you need to concentrate. What does that mean?"

"First I need to be in a position of comfort and safety."

Pete chuckled. "All you got is that chair, miss, and you're safe so long as you don't get any stupid ideas. Do you see that I'm serious?"

"Yes, of course. I know that. I meant that, maybe, you could untie my hands?"

The big man stared down at her a while. Stacey didn't think he was in particularly good shape, but she was slight, and he was big, and a lot of times that's all it took. The chances of her rushing him, even without the gun, were slim. She guessed that Pete came to the same conclusion. He wordlessly fished a small pair of scissors from his bag and snipped the cable ties at her wrist. Stacey flexed and clenched her good hand until life returned to it. She ignored her swollen hand, leaving it resting on the chair arm like a sickly salamander.

The pain was still very loud, but the pills were slowly turning the volume down. She suspected it was fractured, if not broken.

"Thank you," she murmured.

Pete cleared his throat awkwardly. "What else? You need me to cross your palm with silver?"

Stacey looked up to see if she was being mocked and found to her surprise only the usual impassiveness on Pete's face. He was serious. "People normally just pay me in cash," she said. "But I have a PayPal as well."

Pete nodded. "So what else. You're more comfortable now, right?"

The truth was that Stacey's back was seizing up from having been slumped in the chair for God knew how long, and her thighs were raw and itchy from the dried-in piss. "I'll be fine in a moment."

"But what do you need? To talk to the dead, I mean. Is there stuff you need? I brought some stuff with me." Pete rummaged in his bag again. Stacey noticed that as he did so, he quite thoughtlessly put down the pistol and turned his back to her. Had she been a little more alert, a little more courageous, she could have made a dash for it there and then, taken the fucker's gun and blown the back of his head off.

Yeah, she thought, *and maybe he'd ram that gun so far down my throat he wouldn't even need to pull the trigger to fill my ass with lead.*

"Here." Pete turned around and offered her something. It was a teacup. Dainty and elegant, and painted with what looked like a summer scene from Victorian England. She took it in her good hand and looked carefully at it. A man and woman dressed in equally ridiculous finery walked arm in arm across a rolling dale, while in the distance a steam train lay in frozen majesty upon an arched bridge.

"This was your mother's," Stacey said, confidently. She

never asked a question when she could make a statement. That was one of the small but important tricks of the trade.

Pete nodded. "You need this to focus on, right? To make a connection?"

Stacey nodded. "An item of importance or great sentimentality to the past is useful when calling out to them." She decided then, to gently test her luck. "However, the surest way to make a connection is to commune in the residence of the passed, or a place for which they had great affection."

Pete stared down at her for a long while, but Stacey had mastered her poker face years since. "We can't do that," he said. "Will the cup be enough?" As he spoke, he seemed to notice that his hands were free, and picked up the gun absent-mindedly.

"Yes," Stacey said. "The cup will be fine."

"Okay." Pete stood, and then after a while nodded encouragingly.

Stacey swallowed. "It would help if I had something to focus on. A lit candle, or something to help ease myself into a trance state."

Pete once again sat before her, gun held between his knees. "I don't got a candle. I got a flashlight, though. I can turn it on and set it on the table?"

"That would be helpful, thank you."

Pete stood again, and after a brief amount of rummaging he set a small Maglite on its end, its weak beam shining toward the ceiling. "That okay?"

"Yes. That's fine."

Pete sat before her again, eyes never leaving her face.

Stacey hesitated.

"Need something else?" Pete's voice began to take on the edge of menace again. "Need to play some fucking whale music or something? Need me to play those little finger cymbals for you?"

Stacey shook her head, composing herself. She spoke in the soothing anywhere-but-here accent she had used to put countless old widows at ease. "No, Pete. Everything you've done is fine, thank you. I just need to know..." Stacey met the man's gaze, channeling as much empathy and sincerity into her expression as she could. "Why did you kidnap me? If you wanted to talk with your mother, you could have come to me at any time. I would have helped you. You don't need to do any of this, we can—"

Pete very slowly put the pistol against Stacey's forehead and left it there for uncountable seconds while her voice trailed off into a shuddering exhalation. "You're the psychic, right?" he said. "You tell me."

"That's not how it works."

"Sure it is! You got a spirit guide, right? He knows all kinds of shit. Probably knows what I had for breakfast. Ask him what I had for breakfast today."

Stacey looked down, desperately trying to filter out the sensation of cold metal in the center of her forehead. "My guide sees and knows the paths of the departed, those they have touched with their loss. They leave a shape on those they leave behind. Yours was very clear." She closed her eyes and tried her luck again, quietly amazed at her own courage. "She left you very recently."

Her head bobbed forward slightly as the pressure of the pistol was taken away. She opened her eyes and felt something like triumph when she realized that Pete had tears in his eyes. When he spoke, he spoke with a cracked voice. "You're damn right they leave a shape. You're damn right they do."

Stacey's heart thumped in her chest, but it wasn't the rush of fear anymore. This was the confident buzz of someone who was leading the race, her rivals falling away behind her. It didn't matter how tough or smart you were—grief made people soft, and hope made them stupid. She decided to press her advantage, such as it was. "If this is why you brought me here, to talk to your mother, I need to know, what is it you want? What is it you hope to find?"

Pete frowned. "How can you ask me that? She's my mom! I need to know..."

"I know, I know that. But sometimes we don't find the answers we seek. Sometimes the only peace we can find is in letting go of the questions. If your mother is out there, she may not have the answers you need and I know it must upset her so to see you in torment."

"Wait... What do you mean 'if'?"

Stacey carefully placed the teacup on her lap and reached out a hand. Pete flinched the pistol back and then looked puzzled at her hand on his knee. Stacey did not break eye contact. "You are the last link she has to the physical realm, and her bond with you is strongest. If you seek her with fear and confusion in your heart, fear and confusion is all she will be able to feel. In order to commune with your mother, you must be at peace. You must be calm. You must let go of your suspicion, and your anger."

Pete looked at her hand and then at the gun.

"It's okay," Stacey said. "You can keep hold of that if you need it. I don't mind. But you must open your heart. You must trust me."

Pete's jaw stiffened and then shook. His eyes shone wetly in the dark. "Then show me," he whispered. "Show me she's out there."

Stacey nodded. Pete held the gun, true, but she was feeling more and more as though she was the one in charge of the situation. This was her arena, and she was running the show.

Careful, girl, she thought. *Don't get cocky. That's a three-hundred-pound kidnapper with a firearm in front of you, not some whiny housewife looking to be forgiven for putting her dad in a home.*

She looked down at the cup. There was a chip in the rim and a tea stain around the inside. No. She closed her eyes and sniffed a slow breath into her nose. Not tea, coffee. This was a decorative teacup, meant as a souvenir, but the owner had used it often. What else? Now that her eyes had adjusted to the darkness (and with the help of the Maglite,) she could see that the pristine porcelain of the handle was marred a yellowy color. A smoker, then?

These were minor truths, meaning nothing in themselves, but it was all ammunition. She took all she could from the mug, but what about Pete? What had she picked up from him so far? A young man who had probably lived with his mother, and judging by the state of him now, had no one else. This was it. Now the curtain went up. Now the show truly began.

She closed her eyes and spoke in soft, reassuring tones. "With heart and mind, I am reaching out. With guided hand, I am reaching out. Out into the other world, into the after, where the lights and echoes of who we are live on, always. I am reaching out. I am seeking."

Stacey, now very much Madame Shahrazad, paused a moment. Pete made no noise. When an audience was rapt, was fully hooked, there was this peculiar kind of silence, a reverent hush reserved for funeral homes and hospital beds. She felt that quiet now and wrapped it around herself like a comforter.

She creased her brow in a delicate frown. "I see something... a figure..."

"Yes?" Pete's voice was little more than a gasp.

"She sits in the sunlight, smoking a cigarette. Drinking coffee in the afternoon. She smiles, but there is pain in her eyes... Peter. Peter is this your mother?"

There was no reply.

Stacey let a smile spread over her face. "Even through the pain she always had a smile, especially for you. You were the most she had in the world. She was always glad you were there for her. She knows that it was hard sometimes..." She tested her luck once more. "...without your father, it was hard sometimes. Is that true, Peter?"

There was an empty quiet, and then, "Yes."

She had him. She could feel it. But now came the tricky part.

"I'm getting a name...it's not clear...I'm losing the image a little...a name with an M...an Mmmm... a nammme..."

"Her last name was Marshall. Her maiden name, I mean," Pete said.

Stacey resisted the urge to breathe a sigh of relief. She had long ago memorized a list of the most common names in Florida for men and women, over several generations. Someone old enough to be Pete's mother was a high possibility for Emily, or Amy. Guessing the maiden name had been a happy bonus, but the fact that Pete had thought to clarify it as a maiden name also gave her more ammunition.

"She never took her maiden name, though. After your dad...left you both."

"No. She wouldn't do that. She loved my dad, very much."

More ammo. No deadbeat dad skipping out on mommy and baby. This was a confirmed loss, another juicy tidbit dropped by Pete without realizing.

She continued seamlessly. "But she always had you, and she was so grateful for that, Pete. So grateful."

There was a wet sniffle. She was winning him around. Whatever problem this psycho had, he wasn't lying about needing to talk to his mom. He was buying into it. And once they bought into it, everything else was gravy.

"Ask her why she did it, then," said Pete, suddenly.

Stacey froze for just a moment. She preferred to guide the questions of her clients towards the safety of vague but satisfying answers. She couldn't let Pete back into a position of control, not now. She let another frown settle on her brow.

"She...she wants to say something... She has a message..."

"Yes?"

"She says...she says that she loves you...and that she's sorry. Oh, she's so sorry, Pete."

"For what?"

"She's sorry for leaving you. She wishes she could have stayed longer. It breaks her heart to know you're so sad."

There was a pause and more quiet. But it was not the soft reverent quiet that Madame Shahrazad thrived in. She heard Pete shuffle in his chair. "Then ask her why she did it," he said. "If she's so goddamned sorry, ask her why she did it."

Stacey coughed to ease her dry throat. "None of us may truly know when our time has ended on this plane..."

"*She fucking killed herself, you stupid bitch. Of course she knew!*"

At this point Stacey dared not open her eyes. To do so would be to break the spell, to dispel Madame Shahrazad and leave just Stacey James, an ageing trailer trash con artist currently sitting in a puddle of her own urine. Her mind raced.

"She knew, perhaps, but she did not understand. And she needs you to understand, Peter. She needs you to understand that when we are in such pain, sometimes our actions are not our own. Sometimes the darkness is so thick that we can't see through it, no matter how much light there is in our lives. It wasn't her fault, Peter, she didn't want to leave you, not really. And it wasn't your fault either. You did all you could, and she needs you to understand that she loves you and is so, so proud of you."

There was silence again, but Stacey suspected she was far from out of the woods.

"Ask her what she made for dinner that night," Pete said, matter-of-factly.

Stacey rolled her head back and moaned a little. It was

something she usually did to add to the ambience, but it was also a handy way to bide some time while she thought. For obvious reasons she usually tried to avoid such specific questions as much as possible. What would an old lady make for her son on the night of her suicide?

"She made your favorite, of course."

"Yeah, no shit. What was it?"

Damn. Stacey rolled her head and moaned again while she thought. How could you guess someone's favorite food? I mean, judging by the size of the guy, it sure wasn't celery. Still, this was definitely a home-cooked meal, he'd said as much, so that ruled out the usual takeout options. "I am seeing a picture. A kitchen. Warm and cozy. A table with two places set. A delicious smell."

"Oh yeah, what smell?"

Stacey thought about what she knew of the man. Big, fair skinned and blond, blue eyes. Racial profiling wasn't something Madame Shahrazad often had to think about, her client base being predominately white, but this guy looked to be about as northern European as they come, and it was surprising how much little cultural biases persisted down the ages. What does a lily-white old lady home cook for her lily-white son?

"It's a salty smell, like beef gravy. There's meat, dark brown and rich, I'm not sure what it's called..."

"Sloppy Joes. She made sloppy Joes."

Stacey nodded and smiled. She'd been going to say meatloaf, which seemed like a safe bet, but Sloppy Joes would do just fine. "That's it. Sloppy Joes. You've loved those ever since you were a kid."

The silence from Pete was longer this time, and Stacey took the opportunity to regain the initiative. "She's so sorry that she never said goodbye to you properly, Pete. But she wants you to know that she's found peace on the other side."

"With my father?"

Stacey let her smile broaden. "That's right. They're together again, and they're both very happy now. She only wishes that you forgive her, Peter, and that you also are able to find peace."

"Yeah, that's what she wanted." There was a crack in Pete's voice, and Stacey knew she had him where she needed him to be. "Ever since he died, she wanted that. I mean, not at first. At first she was just sad, real sad, you know? And I said to her, I said, maybe you should go and see someone, talk to someone, you know? See if it helps. And she did. And for a little while it did help, I guess."

Stacey heard Pete's chair creak as the big man stood up. She resisted peeking through her eyelids.

Pete cleared his throat a little and continued. "But then she started getting worse. Became convinced that my dad was waiting for her, for both of us. That we'd all be together again because my dad was waiting for us in heaven. You see, it seemed some piece of shit psychic was charging her forty bucks a week to tell her that daddy was checking his watch and waiting for her in a better place."

Stacey felt a cold rush in her guts. She opened her eyes to see the barrel of the gun levelled at the tiny spot above her nose.

"Yep," Pete continued. "Week in and week out, telling my old, bereaved mom over and over again what she wanted to hear. Some selfish, know-nothing charlatan asshole telling her that heaven was only a hop, skip, and a jump away. Do you remember her? Do you remember my mom?"

Stacey felt her jaw begin to shake again. Any illusion of control she had felt fell away into black nothing. She did not remember the old woman. Pete's mom could have been any one of hundreds.

Pete pressed the revolver on to Stacey's head, his voice low and husky. "That night she made Sloppy Joes. Not really my favorite, not since I was eight, anyway. But she added a secret ingredient. Crushed an entire packet of her painkillers into it. Just enough to send mother and child out into the next world."

In her desperation, Stacey's mouth seemed to work of its own accord. "That...that must've been what she meant. When she said she was sorry, she must've meant..."

"Your accent is slipping," Pete interrupted. "And if you insult me like that again, I'll break the teeth out of your head."

Stacey wailed, any coherent reply she had scrambled up by fear.

"So, yeah. Mommy dear planned to do us both in and kick start the family reunion early. I'm a big guy, though, so all I got was a trip to the emergency room, and some police officers telling me not to leave town any time soon."

Stacey felt the barrel push once again into her, as though Pete intended to somehow make a hole in her head without even pulling the trigger.

"Please," she screamed. "I'll give you anything you want!"

"Oh really? Will you give me peace, Madame Shahrazad? Will you bring me to peace? Because I'd like that, I really would."

"I'm sorry!" Stacey wailed. Madame Shahrazad was gone, split, leaving plain old Stacey James to pick up the tab. "I don't hurt anyone, I don't do anything illegal. I just tell them it's going to be okay!"

"You lie to the desperate and the weak, and you charge them for the privilege. You feed on hope like a...like a parasite!" Pete spat the last word, spittle flying from his lips.

"I'm sorry!" Whatever clever words Stacey James had in her arsenal, whatever cunning tricks, they had deserted her just as surely as Madame Shahrazad. "I'm sorry, I'm sorry, I'm sorry!"

"I'll just bet you are," Pete said. "Tell me, Madame Shahrazad, fourteenth generation Romany and spiritual advisor. Tell me. I pull this trigger, do you think you're going on to another place? Or do you think you just end, here, in the dark?"

Stacey sobbed uncontrollably now.

"Tell me!" Pete roared.

"I don't know!"

Pete leaned over her, screaming in her face. "*Yes, you do!* Everybody does! Deep down everybody does! Now, tell me: do you think that when I kill you—and bitch *I am* going to kill you—do you think that anybody is waiting for you on the other side?"

Stacey broke down, the barrel of the pistol the only thing keeping her from slumping out of the chair completely. "No! No! There's no one there! There's no one there!"

Pete swallowed loudly and his heavy breath began to slow. "You know, I think you're right," he said. "In fact, I know you're right. See, my mother didn't smoke, and her name didn't have no 'm' in it. That teacup was just some shit I picked up at a yard sale the other day. I knew you were as fake as a two-dollar bill from the start. But I had to be sure, you know? I had to be sure that when you're dead, you're dead and there's nothing else."

Stacey looked up through her streaming eyes and was surprised to see that Pete was crying also, tears running down his face in steady rivulets. The big man looked at her and smiled faintly. "I had to be sure."

Then he put the barrel of the gun to his temple and pulled the trigger.

Stacey screamed, and for a long time she did nothing else but scream.

Flash forward eighteen months and Stacey James is the last lady in the bar, downing another off-brand bourbon and waiting for one of the circling vultures to swoop down and proposition her. She'd go home with him, probably, because letting some strange drunk hump away their issues on her was still better than going home alone, where no amount of investment in locks and bars made her feel secure anymore.

She didn't have to be psychic to see the future. Tomorrow would be another weekday, and she'd wait tables and make small talk and smile at people in the hopes they'd leave her money. She didn't need the money, not yet, but she needed something to keep her out of the house and away from her thoughts.

Stacey had retired Madame Shahrazad some weeks ago, by necessity. Her client base had begun to drop off, partly down to the fact that some small-town reporter had had a field day with the details of her case. Thanks to Florida criminal reporting law, every detail of how and why she'd been kidnapped had made it on to a popular true crime website. She was famous now, but not in any way she'd wanted to be.

While most of her regulars had abandoned her, she'd still had some clients, and maybe if she'd kept at it, she could've bounced back again. But now, every time she closed her eyes to commune with the spirits, she was convinced that when she opened them again, the sweet old lady looking up at her with hope-filled eyes would be gone, and the barrel of a gun would be waiting for her.

Stacey James had never believed in an afterlife, but she'd since found out that this didn't mean there weren't ghosts that could haunt you.

She looked up from her drink and was dully surprised to

see that one of the vultures had settled into the opposite end of her table and was talking to her about something. It didn't matter what. She smiled, and nodded, and when he took her hand and led her to the taxi, she went without a word.

Later, the slick beery smell of his sweat on her skin, and the low rumble of his snores mercifully keeping the quiet at bay, she sat up in bed, her arms crossed against her breasts. She looked into the dark and thought about the same thing she thought about every night. She had always known that there was no afterlife, and that nobody was waiting for her on the other side. Now, though, when the hours were small and the sun was a lifetime away, she found herself terrified that somebody was.

She had made a healthy living talking to the dead. Now, it seemed, they were beginning to talk back.

forgotten promises

I often think about the right to die. Yes, I know this is a terrible ice breaker at parties, but it's true. Terry Pratchett was a hero to me in life, and also in the way he handled death (please do look up *Shaking Hands with Death*, if you don't know what I mean.)

The right to clock out on your own terms seems only fair to me, and, in a way, courageous. That you have to make the decision while you're still mentally able to enjoy life seems more courageous still. After all, if you don't take the decision, would you really want anyone to? No. That's too much a burden for those you love, and too much satisfaction for your enemies. This little sci-fi piece came to me while I was standing alone at a party, wondering why people were avoiding me.

forgotten promises

GEOFFREY HAMILTON OPENED his eyes and was confused. Had he missed his alarm? Was he late for work? Was it a Saturday? Where was Michelle?

These were all reflex questions. He had not set an alarm. He had not been to work in twenty-five years. One day was much the same as another. And Michelle had died too, too young.

He had fallen asleep in his chair (his wheelchair, he knew that much. They moved him around into the light like a flower, a dandelion probably, all white and fragile.) He was dimly aware of the shape of his body, slouched and malleable, settled like Jell-O into a mold.

He looked around, his eyes the last reliable component of his seared and oxidized circuitry. The walls and the door and the sink. The steady, electric yellow of the overhead light. He often woke up to the plain cream of his living space, empty and sterile and reassuring as a box of tissues. Sometimes he woke up to faces. The shiny black face of the smiling nurse whose name he couldn't remember, or the lopsided grin and scraggy beard of a man he suspected was also a nurse. They had a lot of male nurses now.

Sometimes he woke up to faces that were hopeful, searching, but ultimately unfamiliar. They held his hand, these faces. Were they his children? Impossible. His little girl was only eight, or twelve or thirty-five, and his son was only a boy, or a man, or a father himself.

He couldn't remember. Couldn't get it straight. Couldn't even remember why he couldn't remember. It was to Geoffrey as though waking from a convincing dream, unsure of that which was plucked from memory and that which was woven from fantasy.

Each day his life was presented to him as a series of rushes, with no master edit to give context or meaning.

Each day Geoffrey stared dumbly at the pieces of his identity, shattered like broken glass, scattered and strewn across a linoleum floor, and he wondered, dimly wondered, who he was.

Today he woke up to faces. They were unfamiliar.

Two men, smiling. Reassuring smiles hovering above their plain and reassuring neckties. Sensible suits. They seemed to Geoffrey like Mormons, or salesman, or funeral directors.

One spoke. The older one with a thin gray moustache and immaculately oiled hair. "Mr. Hamilton?"

Geoffrey stared. He opened his dry mouth and rumbled a few incoherent syllables.

The younger face, pale and pointed behind neat little glasses, tapped impatiently at the tablet he was carrying. "He...uh...he has an ID tag on his wrist. See?"

The older man held up a hand slightly, and the younger cleared his throat and stood straighter.

"Mr. Hamilton?"Geoffrey cracked a few syllables again, coughed, and managed to speak. "Yes. Me."

The man with the silver moustache nodded, respectfully. "My colleague and I are from the Floe Foundation, and if you don't mind, we'd like to play you a special personal message?"

Geoffrey stared watery eyed from one man to another. Eventually, he nodded.

The man turned to his colleague. "Mr. Harima, if you would?"

The younger man, Harima, nodded curtly and produced a small black bar from inside his suit. With a flick of his wrist, it became a long flexible pole, which he set down in front of Geoffrey. Then he attached the tablet, pushed a section of the onyx screen, and stepped away.

Geoffrey stared dumbly as the screen came to life, revealing another face.

He knew this face, though. It was his own.

Surely he would never forget that. A face he shaved every day for so many, many years. The face that watched him carefully when he fixed his hair, straightened his collar, or tentatively examined a pimple.

But, perhaps not his own face. Not as it was now. No dandelion tufts of hair around his ears, no quiet desperation in the eyes, no slack jaw or wrinkled neck. This was Geoffrey younger and stronger. Late middle age, perhaps, before autumn, brittle as it was, snapped and shattered under the weight of winter.

The Geoffrey in the screen cleared his throat, his eyes tracking back and forth over something unseen. He spoke:

"I, Geoffrey Gray Hamilton, being of sound mind and under no duress, hereby acknowledge the agreement made with the Floe Foundation on this...uh..."

Screen Geoffrey held up a document, signed and stamped many times. "...the sixth of July, in the year 2016."

Geoffrey furrowed his brow, puzzled. How long ago was 2016? What year was it now? He did not remember this video, this document. He thought he remembered something about the Floe Foundation, but... no wait. The man with the silver moustache had said that, hadn't he? Geoffrey looked up and made a wordless noise.

The man with the silver moustache nodded patiently and gestured back to the screen. "Please," he said. "It won't take a minute."

Geoffrey nodded slightly and turned back to his younger self on the screen, who was saying a lot of unfamiliar words. Legal jargon.

"...and furthermore that no third party transactionally connected to the event is either aware of or culpable in this arrangement. And that no next of kin shall be informed of this arrangement. And in the context of this arrangement and that the listed criteria are met, I fully and completely give my permission for the Floe Foundation to administer a controlled air injection into my pulmonary vein until I am medically deceased."

Geoffrey blinked at his impassive, younger reflection. His younger self seemed quite unperturbed by what he just said. Impatient, almost. As though the weighty tombstone of the statement was in fact just a Styrofoam Halloween prop.

The younger Geoffrey looked off screen. "Is that...?" He stared for a while, listening to an unheard voice. "Well...sure, I guess." He then turned back to face the camera and cleared his throat again. "Apparently I'm supposed to say something reassuring to you...me...I guess. In case you...forgot why you're doing this."

Geoffrey—Geoffrey in the here and now—nodded slowly, temporarily forgetting how separated he was from this other version of himself by years unknown.

"First of all—the kids ain't ever gonna know. This is gonna look like natural causes. No shame, no guilt. They'll be fine. Second... I mean. I don't have to explain this to you, do I? You remember Meemaw, right? Do you want to end up like that?"

Geoffrey nodded. He did remember Meemaw, vaguely. He

had liked her. Liked the way she cooed and smiled at him, and the way the other grownups treated her with a patient softness they rarely reserved for one another. Had he wanted to end up like that? Had he even thought about it? He supposed he must have, once.

He realized that he, the other him, was still speaking.

"And, hell, you've had a good run. I mean, probably." He chuckled. "Knowing my luck, I'll walk out of here and get hit by a bus. But if we make it that far that the disease becomes a problem... I don't want this on anyone else's shoulders. A man should be able to say when enough is enough, don't you think? I mean, that's fair, right? I think that's fair."

Geoffrey nodded. It sounded fair, he supposed.

"So...uh..." The other Geoffrey looked uncomfortable. "I don't know what to say. It hasn't always been easy. I mean, that's got to be true for everyone, right? But there were good times. Real good times. I guess...heh. I guess I'll see you later."

The screen went dark.

"Mr. Hamilton?"

Geoffrey looked up at the man with the silver moustache. His face was impassive. Professional. But not unkind. "Did you understand all that, Mr. Hamilton?"

Geoffrey thought. He thought maybe he did. Or maybe not. It was already slipping. But he nodded and smiled. These faces seemed like nice faces.

"Mr. Harima, if you would?" The younger man, who had finished retrieving the tablet and stand, produced a small, black bag. In a moment his hands were adorned with white rubber gloves, his sleeves rolled up. In a moment more, he was carefully eyeing a syringe.

Geoffrey turned as he felt a hand take his. The face, the older face, was creased with gentle reassurance. "This will only take a moment, Mr. Hamilton."

Geoffrey felt a spike of fear, but that quickly turned into

confusion. Where did he know this man with the silver moustache from? Was it a friend? A nurse? His brother?

He tried to recall, tried to find the face somewhere in his life, but once again the moments were jumbled and scattered before him, fragmented like broken glass across a linoleum floor.

A baby in his arms, face screwed up in sleep.

A woman beneath him breathing his name.

A boy becoming a man, finding his hand at a funeral service.

His mother, smiling.

All of them scattered, out of time and place.

Geoffrey felt a painful sensation in his arm, and the world began to dim, but the pieces, those pieces scattered before him, became sharper, clearer.

A toddler squeezing her arms around his neck.

An old movie on a cold day with a head warm against his shoulder.

The bright playing fields of eternal summers.

Geoffrey realized that these pieces were not glass at all. Not even broken. They were jewels. Each tiny and precious and gleaming against the dark.

Not broken at all.

Mr. Aukland stepped into the light, quietly relieved as usual. Early in his career he'd struggled through an array of emotions once a job was done. But these days, with so many under his belt, it was always just quiet relief.

The old man, Mr. Hamilton, had gone out without struggle, which was a mercy. His policy was paid out in full, which was appropriate. And it was a comfort that any nearest and dearest he had left would think he passed quietly in his sleep.

Around Mr. Aukland, the noise of gentle traffic and bird song was a welcome counterpoint to the cloying hush of the nursing home. The sun felt good on his face. The breeze felt like a welcome back.

Behind him, Mr. Harima stepped out and stretched. "Are we on schedule?" he said, casually.

"Ahead actually," said Mr. Aukland. "We can stop for a bite if you're hungry."

"Nah," said Harimo. "Let's cruise on through it. See if we can finish early."

Aukland felt a bristle of annoyance but tried not to show it as they walked to their company car, a non-descript black Toyota. "You got somewhere to be?" he asked, casually.

Harima considered, briefly. "Nah, not really. Just get it done and enjoy the day, why not?"

Aukland shrugged. "It takes as long as it takes."

They entered the car, Aukland wincing slightly as his hip twinged, a more and more common experience that seemed not to dull with repetition. He started the silent electric engine and pulled the car out into the wide roads. They drove together in silence for a few miles. Aukland had only been working with Harima for a few months, but that was long enough to know when his partner's mind was occupied.

"You stuck on something?" he offered.

Harima shook his head, and then took a short, sharp breath. "The worst part of all this is playing them that damn video," he said, his words rushing out.

"Really?" Aukland replied, slowly. "That's the worst part for you?"

"Yeah." Harima sighed. "It's, like, what's the point? They never seem to understand what it is they're seeing, and when they do, they get upset. Why even bother? A contract's a contract, whether you remember signing it or not."

"It's a kindness," Aukland said, flatly.

Harima arched an eyebrow. "You think so? How so?"

"Respect, I guess. Some part of them sees it, I think. It's just respectful."

"Well, you do you," Harima said. "Me? I wouldn't give a shit."

"That so?"

"It doesn't make a difference. If your number's up, your number's up."

Auckland nodded, and they drove a while in silence. His hip twinged again, and he shuffled in his seat to redistribute his weight.

"What do you think's a good age?" Auckland said, the words tumbling from his mouth without him really giving them permission.

"What?"

"To punch out? What's a good age? For you, I mean."

Harima considered. "Pfft, I don't know. With my genes... eighty-five I guess?"

"Eighty-five?"

"Yeah, sure. I mean, it's all down-hill from there, right? Can't wipe your own ass, can't eat the food you like, can barely see your favorite shows."

"So, you'd be happy to get ended at eighty-five?"

"Sure."

Aukland snorted. "You want I should ask you again when you're eighty-four?"

Harima snorted back. "Hell, I don't know."

"Do you think anyone does? Really?"

"Cut that out, man," Harima snapped. He turned his face from his partner, staring instead out of the window at the passing world. A young girl in a red dress skipped in her front yard. She was there and then she wasn't. "You know what we do," Harima continued, slowly. "These people give us very clear stipulations. We're doing them a mercy and you know it. A mercy they asked for. They made a promise..."

"I know it," Aukland said, nodding gently. "A promise they may have forgotten. That they may need reminded of. So, I show them the video, and I hold their hand. Seems like respect is the last thing you can give someone, I reckon."

"Yeah." Harima looked out of the window at the passing houses. "Yeah, maybe."

They drove on farther down the road before turning into the drive of another nursing home, where the quiet and the forgotten promises waited for them.

la petit rouge

Okay, maybe a something a little less depressing now. But only a little. I was invited by Johnathon Yanez to contribute to the *Beyond Midnight* anthology where the only unifying theme was "bad ass." I decided it was a perfect opportunity to follow that trend where people do adult takes on fairytale stories. It started as a parody, but I found myself leaning into the action and world building.

The great thing about short stories is you can write a lot of checks you don't have to cash, but who knows, maybe one day I'll write more about the GRIMs and their battles in the fae-pocalypse. It's good to get a little bad ass now and then.

la petit rouge

HUNTER STOMPED through the streets of Gray City, rain streaming in waterfalls down the broad back of his overcoat. He looked out at the world from the low brim of a sopping fedora, grimacing behind a three-day growth and a jaw like a clenched fist. As usual, Gray City was anything but. The soaking wet concrete reflected the gaudy hot pink and purples of bar and brothel signage, forming a pool of seedy electric that rippled and leaped crazily with every passing footstep.

Hawkers, drunks, and wrong numbers filled the strip known locally as The Scrum, each of them jostling to get to whatever drug, mark, or piece of flesh they craved. But even amongst the panicky tight press of the streets, the crowd parted slightly for Hunter, who projected an aura of menace equivalent to a rottweiler chewing enthusiastically on a hand grenade.

Not all were deterred, however, and a skinny guy dressed in engineer's overalls fell into step alongside him, pulling along a motorized gurney loaded down with coffin-shaped crates.

"Hey, buddy, I got what you need!"

Hunter stopped and looked down at the hawker. Hunter looked down at most people, and usually the way he did so was enough to convey a series of possible futures that were equally and creatively terrible for anyone he was looking at. The skinny guy, to his credit, remained completely undeterred. His face was dominated by a broad and enterprising grin.

"I got what you need, fella!"

Hunter talked with a voice so deep and raspy it was like listening to someone hit a tombstone with another, heavier tombstone. "I doubt that very much, Jack."

"Nah, 'course I do. Check it out!" The engineer flipped open one of the crates. Inside were a series of shapely legs, in all shades and size. Some tattooed, some not. Some clothed in fishnets, or knee-high socks, some nude but for their painted toes. The engineer flipped open another crate, which had a likewise selection of asses.

"I got legs for days and tits that won't quit. Pick and mix your favorites and I'll have the girl of your dreams ready for you in the blink of an eye!" He grinned and held up a motorized socket wrench. He gave the trigger a couple of squeezes, arching his eyebrows in a knowing way with each rev of the motor.

Hunter stared unblinkingly. "Girl of my dreams ain't made of plastic, Jack."

The engineer bristled, sticking out his chin defiantly. "Hey, what do you take me for? These are all high-quality silicone plas-tech, buddy, top of the line. Feels just like the real thing. Hell, better than the real thing!"

Hunter leaned down slightly. "I'm tired of your words. Improve my view and fade away."

Whatever internal dynamo drove the robot pimp's sales banter had apparently overridden his basic survival instinct. He opened another box, this one filled with a variety of beautiful heads, their mouths uniformly opened in a permanent 'o'. "Now, you tell me there's a not a single—"

The robot pimp didn't get to finish his pitch. Hunter

hauled him up by his overalls and slung him like a javelin into the neon sign for a twenty-four-hour porno theater. There was a boom of sparks before a small darkness marred the uninterrupted glare of the Scrum. Amongst the wreck of the signage, a pair of legs twitched a few times and then stopped moving. There were a few screams. And a few laughs.

Hunter moved on, and behind him the crates were looted with piranha-like speed, various legs, torsos, and other appendages carried away in all directions, as though a dozen porn stars had exploded in slow motion.

In any other city there'd have been sirens by now. But Gray City, like most of the new cities, was its own state. Gray City had its own laws, or lack of them, haphazardly enforced by whatever crime syndicate happened to be in control at any given moment. If anyone had cared for the hapless vendor, or justice in general, they wouldn't give the luxury of a siren. Just a knife in the back when you least expected it.

Hunter checked the indicator on his wrist console. The smooth glass dome was a fuzzy pink. The reading was no longer precise enough to indicate a general direction, but the fact that it had yet to turn red suggested he wasn't in any immediate danger. Wandering around until that was the case wasn't an ideal strategy, he knew that from experience. Luckily, he already had a contact. He scanned the busy streets until he saw the restaurant sign.

KNICK KNACK PADDY WOK.

Above the words was a cartoon of what appeared to be a leprechaun wearing a rice-farmer's hat. It was punching a fish.

Ever since the Fairytale of New York, where hundreds of thousands had died, and millions more had been displaced, most of the New Cities had popped up virtually overnight. With no traditions or cultural majorities, fusion cuisine had quickly become the norm. This particular chain specialized in stout flavored wonton soup, and rabbit and potato pad thai.

Hunter's taste buds had long ago been reconfigured chiefly to detect atmospheric poisons, but even he would have thought twice about eating there.

Inside, a dull-eyed chef bent over a huge wok, eliciting steam and smells and the occasional pop of oil. Propped against the service counter was a diminutive man in a brilliant blue suit. The man turned, flashed an easy-going grin, and gave a casual wave. He had the kind of glowing skin that spoke of expensive face creams. Hunter suspected that here was the diplomatic face of the Muffet Sisters Crime Syndicate. The man gestured to his half-finished bowl and spoke in a London accent. "Can I interest you in some soda bread chow mien?"

Hunter shook his head.

The man laughed and extended a hand. "Boy Blue. I'm your contact."

Hunter regarded the hand and fished his ID from his inner coat pocket. Boy Blue took it and examined it, his eyebrows raising slightly.

"Welp, you're a fed alright. Mr. Hunter?"

"Just Hunter."

The server briefly stopped stirring the mess of ingredients in her wok, shooting Hunter a quick nervous glance.

"And GRIM, too?" Boy Blue continued. "I mean, I saw you throw that guy through a wall, my first thought was exosuit, but this..." He made a vague gesture, taking in Hunter's absurd bulk. "This is all cooked up in the lab, huh?"

Hunter nodded. "Genetically Resequenced Infantry."

Boy Blue frowned. "So what does the 'm' stand for?"

"Classified."

"Say no more. So, how should we do this?"

Hunter looked around the cramped eating area. "They just send you, Jack?"

"I'm all you've got I'm afraid. The Sisters are more than

happy to let the feds take care of this. With minimal disruption to the nightlife, if at all possible."

"No guarantees on nightlife disruption. And I prefer to work alone."

"No problem. Last time we had an...uh...incident, we sent in our own heavies. Things got expensive. And messy."

Hunter looked Boy Blue up and down. "So you're not a heavy?"

Boy Blue shifted his shoulders in a manner that suggested, if needs required, he could be so. "Me? Nah. I'm a face. A fixer. I keep the cows out of the corn, so to speak. Something needs to be tidy, I keep it tidy."

"I don't guarantee tidy."

Boy Blue sighed. "So, what do you need from me?"

"A location. And to keep out of my way."

Boy Blue's eyebrows raised ever so slightly. Hunter suspected, for all the man's laid-back attitude, he was no stranger to violence. The irked expression was gone as quickly as it appeared, replaced by a reassuring smile. "No problem. Come on."

Hunter followed Boy Blue's lead into the streets where the rain was beginning to let up a little. He pretended not to notice as the server quickly shut up shop behind them. Ahead of them, the crowd gave the pair even more room than they had given Hunter, speaking volumes about Boy Blue's reputation. One man, a street vendor carrying a bulky tray of glow-in-the-dark butt plugs, launched his wares into the road and dove into the gutter just to get out of their way.

"So," said Blue. "You know what you're dealing with?"

Hunter barely paused. "Class Three concentration of Fae Flora. Likely one vessel."

Blue shrugged. "Don't know nothing about 'Class Three' but, yeah, we think there's only one."

"You've seen it?"

"Nah." The smaller man laughed. "We've seen where it's *been*. It's...uh...not subtle."

"Victims?"

"Yes. Eight. Messy ones."

Hunter's hand went to his hip, where the snub-nosed pistol bulged conspicuously under his trench coat.

Boy Blue turned around. "Before I tell you where to go, I want you to give me a chance to empty the place, yeah? There's a lot of paying customers in there, and paying customers make the world go 'round."

Hunter shook his head. "Can't risk giving it a head's up, Jack. Right now there's one of these things. It goes underground then maybe it starts making more. You want a situation like in Central Europe?"

Boy Blue gave a pained expression. Other than Switzerland, which was now effectively one big military base surrounding the Hadron Collider, Fae vessels were a fact of life in Central Europe. Entire metropolis had transformed, in ten short years, into human no-go areas. Little footage made it back from those areas, with spotter drones being picked out of the air by any number of weird beasts. But the footage that did make it back was enough to keep the funding for Hunter's department well into the billions.

Hunter remembered his induction as a young volunteer, a totally different animal from what he was now. He had sat in a fold-up chair in a dimly lit room with all the other fresh-faced patriots, staring wide-eyed at the projector screen. Images flickered serenely and silently. Physics-defying towers of weird, black stone. Forests of bulbous mushrooms. Cities of glass. And the creatures, the vessels. Maybe once humans, but far beyond that now.

"No one wants that," Boy Blue cut through Hunter's vivid recollection of his previous life. "Sisters say I've got to give you everything you need, but these are *people*, man. They ain't soldiers. Just customers, you know?"

"They're people for now, Jack."

The smaller man held up his hands. "Can you promise me you'll try and get the civilians out of the line of fire?"

Hunter thought for a moment. "No guarantees."

Boy Blue sighed. "Fine." He pointed to a red glowing light farther down the street. "La Petit Rouge. Strip joint. Our intel says that's where it's holding up."

Hunter walked away without a word.

La Petit Rogue had a definite theme. The walls were painted red, the chairs finished in red leather. Every single light was red, picking out the clientele in shades of crimson and black. In the middle of the room was a small stage and pole, where a young woman with gravity-defying breasts writhed and rotated. A redhead of course. The whole joint put Hunter in mind of an open wound.

It didn't take him long to spot his target. He leaned over the bar and ripped out the power cord to the sound system, plunging the venue into an awkward silence. A harried-looking bartender approached, looking strangely officious in his red vest and bowtie.

"Hey, what the fuck do you think you're—" The barman paused as Hunter's snub-nosed pistol suddenly appeared in his face. It wasn't a conventional gun. Its barrel was an inch wide, and its ammo chamber looked like someone had inflated an old-style magnum to cartoon proportions. The bartender didn't know it, but the gun didn't fire bullets. It fired phosphorus rounds. Not that this made much of a difference to the implication.

"Anyone who don't want to get perforated, leave now," Hunter growled.

The clientele rushed for the doors and the strippers ran

after them, holding down their breasts and leaving their high heels in their wake.

After the brief and busy commotion, only one person remained. A woman of aging years sat alone in a booth, nursing a tumbler of rum. She looked up at Hunter and gestured for him to take a seat. Hunter did so, keeping the snub nose trained on her with mechanical precision.

"I wondered how long before they sent someone like you," the old woman said.

Hunter spoke dispassionately. "Professor Charlotte Mackenzie. A.K.A Terrice Fairbright. A.K.A Felicity Brown."

The woman nodded. "That's me. The first one, at any rate."

"I've been instructed to take you in for processing. If you resist in any way, I am instructed to use lethal force."

Charlotte sipped her drink. "Dead or alive, huh?"

"Alive is preferable, but not required."

The old lady sneered, a seemingly involuntary action. "Processing? Now, what could you possibly hope to process from an old gal like me?"

Hunter gestured to his wrist console. It was difficult to make out the deep red in the lighting of La Petit Rouge, but he gestured to it anyway. "You're a Class Three Fae Vessel. Your presence in the United States is a crime."

"My, my. A class three, ay? Is that what they're calling me?"

"Come quietly or die here, Jack, that's as much of a negotiation as you're going to get."

The woman nodded. "Do you know how I became exposed to the Fae?"

"Not my concern."

She fixed him a hard glare. "I'll tell you regardless. I'm old, son, and when you're old, you learn to take your time." As if to illustrate her point, she took a long, slow sip of the rum. "I was there at the start, you know. When the breach first happened. Oh, we were all so excited about the Fae Flora to begin with. The medical applications alone could have transformed the lives of millions. But, of course, the real money came in when the military applications became apparent."

Hunter said nothing. He didn't need to make any special effort to keep his expression unreadable.

The lady took another sip of her drink, her hand barely shaking. "Of course, by the time I realized I'd become a...what did you call it, a vessel? A vessel, yes. Not quite the accurate term, but it'll do, I suppose. By the time I realized I was gestating Fae Flora, the writing was on the wall. I knew I had to go on the run. I figured they'd kill me out of fear. If I was lucky. Keep me for study if I wasn't."

"They would have been right to," said Hunter. "Kill you, I mean."

If the statement upset Charlotte at all, she didn't let it show. "You know what I learned, from my experiences? From my own self-study? At first I was petrified, of course. I kept waiting for my mind to go, to turn into a deranged beast. I thought that was what would happen."

"You saying it didn't?"

Charlotte shook her head. "That's what I learned. The flora is not evil, son. It's not anything like us. It's like...a fungus. It doesn't want to rule the world. It just wants to live."

"Not evil?" Hunter's mind flashed back to the induction video, to the countless bloody aftermath of Fae encounters he'd witnessed since. "Tell that to Munich. Tell that to Vienna. Hell, tell it to Belgium."

"The Fae is power, son, no doubt." Charlotte looked up from her drink and gazed impassively into Hunter's eyes. "And when people get power...well, you must know. Look at you."

Hunter cocked back the hammer on his snub nose. "I ain't

nothing like you, Jack. You've killed eight people that we know of."

"A lady's entitled to defend herself, wouldn't you say?"

"You ain't a lady."

Charlotte nodded and looked down at her drink, idly passing the tumbler from hand to hand. "So. You want to take me in for processing? Can you tell me what that entails, exactly?"

"Classified."

"I figured as much." She slowly slid the tumbler away from herself. "I was there at the start. I saw what we did to people when they started to change. When humans get scared, they'll justify anything. Anything. So you'll forgive me if I pass up on your offer of 'processing.'"

She moved quicker than Hunter's trigger finger, and Hunter's trigger finger moved pretty damn quick. There was the click of the hammer, the boom of the pistol, and the whoosh as the leather couch erupted into a white-hot ball of fire. But Charlotte had dived clear and was already heading to a door marked 'STAFF', darting across the room with impossible grace. Hunter didn't hesitate, he ripped the booth table from its mooring and slung it like a discus. It smashed into the wall inches from the retreating figure's head.

Hunter charged through the room, chairs and tables exploding out of his path. Fae could be fast, but he had been reconfigured with muscle fiber like steel cable, and for all that he was big, he moved liked the wind.

Beyond the door was a concrete staircase ascending into the dark. Hunter bounded up, five steps at a time, his gun leading the way. The staircase turned in on itself, and he crashed into walls as he negotiated the tight corners. He could just about see a flit of movement above him, rounding the upper corners as he rounded the lowers.

Hunter's mind was racing as fast as his body. He tried to

prepare for what he might be up against, but it wasn't easy. Fae came in many forms. Class Three was only a signifier of the concentration of flora within the vessel, not an indicator of its form. He'd put away his fair share of lower class, those whose infestations only granted them meager abilities: gnolls and trolls and such. And he'd never seen a Class Six: the impossible witches and wizards that were able to mold the world to their mad designs. Not many had and had lived to tell about it. But Class Three was tricky and compromised the most varied entries in the department's ever-expanding bestiary. Psiren, banshee, vampire. Maybe something yet to be cataloged. Whatever it was, he aimed to kill it.

The stairs finally ended in a heavy metal door, which Hunter kicked from its hinges without slowing. He burst out into the night, the cool air and muted noise giving him some indication of how high above the streets the rooftop was. He slowly tracked his gun from shadow to shadow.

He felt no fear. No increase in his heart rate. His adrenal management had been resequenced along with the rest of his body. GRIMs typically existed in a constant state of low-level aggression, fear being a luxury they could ill afford.

There was cover on the roof. Too much. Vents and air conditioning units. Chimneys and storage sheds. There were more places to hide on the roof than there had been on the ground floor.

Hunter heard the shift of body on concrete, but it was not warning enough. A loud snarl coincided with a heady weight slamming into his back and knocking him to the ground. The sensation of hot breath on the back of his head was immediately superseded by the sensation of wet teeth digging into his neck. Hunter bucked his body before the bite could find real purchase, and a dark shape tumbled out to the concrete before him. He chased it with two phosphorous rounds and the rooftop came alive with painful white light.

Moving in a slow circle, Hunter held an arm near his face defensively. He kept his gun hand behind him, conscious the next attack could come from any direction. He blinked rapidly, trying to dispel the purple glaring after-images that swarmed his vision. He had only captured the briefest glance at the creature before it had slipped back into shadows but recognized it as a Dire Wolf. Something not unlike an earth wolf, but the nearest approximation in the Fae Flora's genetic memory. Bigger, faster, meaner.

When the breach had happened—and before the UN had buried it under a thousand tons of concrete and steel—scientists had been able to run dozens of satellite arrays into the new world beyond, finding only empty plains of barren earth under unfamiliar stars. No structures, no forests, nothing. They hadn't found much animal life. Or at least, they thought they hadn't—but that had been before they'd realized the Fae Flora was far more than benign glittery spore.

The world had been home to only a few hundred beasts, impossible leviathans that would later become known as Mega Vessels, or Class X. Those weird marauding giants, stomping around on skyscraper legs, or floating like small moons, simply traveled silently and aimlessly, conspicuously avoiding one another's territory. There had been no smaller lifeforms. And yet, once they had infiltrated Earth, the Fae Flora constantly transformed vessels into creatures that were alien. The leading hypothesis was that the Mega Vessels were the end game of a peculiar evolutionary race, but that the Fae remembered more economic shapes from their past, suitable for smaller concentrations of flora, and mutated their vessels accordingly.

Dire Wolves were common in Class Two and Three concentrations, with less common Class Four variants. An efficient predator shape, without any needless complications. Just a hide that could stop small arms fire and a bite that could tear a fender from a truck. Traits that may have worried a body that hadn't been rebuilt for war on a cellular level. Hunter concluded that taking this one alive might not be an option after all.

"You know," Hunter said. "This won't end well for you. Ain't no way off this roof 'cept through me."

Silence.

"Hand yourself in. We'll get a leash on you. Hell, if you're going to go, there are more comfortable ways than me burning you to ash."

"It would be quick, though." The voice was deeper, more guttural, but still recognizable as the Professor's.

Hunter was surprised. In its mutative state, a vessel rarely spoke. At least not to him. He strained his ears, trying to pin down where the voice was coming from, but the acoustics of the roof were strangely flat. The voice seemed like it could be coming from anywhere.

"Quicker than having the flora extracted," the beast continued. "You know it's fused with me on a microscopic level. You know it dies if I die. You know I have to be alive for them to extract it."

Hunter shrugged. "Not my department."

"And then what? What do they do with all that power? Some kind of weapon? Some kind of lab freak, like you? Tell me, what is the value in destroying one monster to fuel another?"

Hunter wasn't given a chance to reply. There was a sudden burning pressure on his gun hand as the Dire Wolf's jaws ripped into it, sending his snub nose pistol skittering across the rooftop. He dived toward it, but the wolf barreled into him, hurtling him over the roof edge. Hunter reached out instinctively with one hand, his fingers practically forcing their way into the concrete lip of the roof. He dangled for barely a second above the whining streets, before swinging himself back onto the rooftop. A second was all it took. The beast stood, the snub nose held between two of its clawed fingers like something unpleasant picked from a meal. The beast, without breaking eye contact, threw the weapon over the roof.

Hunter nodded slowly, taking in the grinning beast before him. It was a mass of matted black hair, broad in the shoulder and narrow in the hip. It stood on meaty hind legs, its forelegs somewhere between ape and canine, and finished in heavy-looking claws. Its head was similar to a conventional wolf's, its white teeth, red tongue, and yellow eyes the only color on the dark roof. The thing tilted its head and spoke.

"A little more even, now. A little more fair."

Hunter reflected that the Dire Wolf did not actually speak with its animal muzzle, which remained open and still, but that the words seemed to come from deep within the throat, as though the beast had swallowed the old lady and she was calling out from its guts. Hunter cracked his knuckles, inconspicuously assessing the wound on his right arm. His sleeve had turned deep crimson. The bite had shredded tendon. He figured he had at most sixty percent of his original grip strength. No matter.

"Don't need a gun to end this, Jack," he said.

The Dire Wolf tensed and charged forward in a blur of movement. Hunter was ready, he swung a heavy front kick that caught the beast in the neck and sent it sprawling with a high-pitched yelp. Hunter didn't relent—to allow such a quick opponent even a second to reorientate itself would be folly. He leapt forward and hammered both his fists down on the monster's ribcage. Jaws snapped at his hands, and he moved back just in time to avoid losing a finger or two. Now that his fists were his primary weapon, he needed to be mindful of them.

His hesitation was all his opponent needed. The Dire Wolf leapt at head height, jaws meaning to close on Hunter's throat. Hunter ducked and shifted into a grapple, transforming the beast's leap into a bone-crushing throw. He stomped down at the prone animal, concentrating on the ribs, hoping to break and wind the thing.

The Dire Wolf twisted and spun, and Hunter became aware of a wet sensation on his thigh. The thing had slashed his femoral artery with its claw. It was a studied, intelligent attack that—if not for the smart coagulant agent that ran through Hunter's veins—would have ended him in minutes. Still, even with all his advantages, Hunter realized he had underestimated his opponent. Professor Charlotte Mackenzie knew how to hurt a man.

He staggered back. Pain and fatigue were distant things to him, but he could feel them there, watching. He raised his guard, wary of finding himself on the defensive. The Dire Wolf readied itself on its haunches. If Hunter's attacks had slowed it in any way, the beast wasn't letting it show. It suddenly reared up on its hind legs and swung a claw. Hunter blocked with his left arm and simultaneously sent a meaty right uppercut into the vulnerable space just below the creature's sternum. It staggered back, but not without taking a slice out of Hunter's defending arm.

Hunter tried to use the moment to press what he hoped would be an unexpected attack, rushing in to tackle the beast. He was too slow. The Dire Wolf sank its teeth into his shoulder and pinned him to the ground. He let out a grunt of frustration as he heard bone snap and felt his own blood splash against his neck. He managed to edge his feet between him and his attacker, and launch the beast away from him.

He staggered to his feet, knowing that another attack like that would be the end of him. The beast regarded him curiously, sat on its haunches, apparently confident that Hunter no longer presented a serious threat.

"You should have left me alone," said the Wolf.

Hunter shook his head. "So you can carry on chewing up

the locals?"

"Criminals," it said. "Animals."

"Not your place to say, Jack."

"Because I don't have a badge?"

Hunter nodded. "Basically."

The beast raised up on its hind legs again, ready to pounce. "I want you to know I don't take any pleasure in what I'm about to do."

"I want you to know something too..." said Hunter.

"Oh?"

Hunter concentrated, allowing his eyes to close. He accessed those memories that did not belong to him. Not the memories of the young patriot, not the memories of the hardened inhuman agent. The memories of the other world. The possibilities of an alien universe.

He spoke the word of power. Light streamed from his eyes and fingertips.

The Dire Wolf had time to recognize what was happening, and its eyes widened in dumb terror. Then its head snapped back, a dual scream of woman and animal erupted from its maw. Its flesh began to ripple and undulated. Gouts of gore squirted from its mouth and anus. Bones snapped loudly as the thing folded in on itself, flesh ripping as it melted into a steaming mound of protoplasm and fur.

The scream echoed in Hunter's ears, and he collapsed to his knees, fatigued beyond even his own monstrous endurance. He sat there for some minutes until the sound of a throat clearing caught his attention. He looked up to see Boy Blue leaned causally against the rooftop's entrance.

"So, that's what the 'M' stands for, huh?"

Hunter said nothing.

"Mystic?" Boy Blue continued. "Mage? Magic? It all sounds goofy as shit, but I don't know any other words for what you just did."

Hunter struggled to his feet. "You don't need no words for it, Jack, 'cause it didn't happen. You didn't see anything."

"I saw you turn that thing inside out without touching it. And I saw that light. First time I've seen it outside of drone footage. That was Fae. You got Fae in you. Lots of it."

"Not exactly."

Boy Blue's calm demeanor transformed into a snarl. "The Sisters called you in because we want this bullshit off of our streets, man. We're supposed to be co-operating! There's supposed to be trust! If you guys are using that scary shit, too, then what's the difference between you and them?"

Hunter thought for a moment. "I got a badge," he concluded.

He shoved past Boy Blue and made his way to the exit. Hunter figured he had about fifteen minutes until he collapsed. Enough time to organize an E-vac and wake up in a nice, cool medical facility. His injuries would be death or a lifetime of disability for most, but he knew the department would have him patched up like new in a couple of weeks. Hunter stopped, remembering something.

"Those people that thing killed. Who were they?"

Boy Blue shrugged. "Couple of gang members. Couple of small-time street hustlers. Couple of no names. Probably just muggers."

"Criminals?"

Boy Blue frowned and gestured around the skyline of Gray City. "Ain't we all?"

Hunter said nothing.

"What difference does that make anyway? Why does it matter?" said Blue.

Hunter limped slowly through the door, into the darkness beyond.

"Guess it don't matter anything, Jack. Nothing at all."

everyone you love will be eaten by wolves

The following story was written more or less off-the-cuff when an anthology I was involved in needed a couple of thousand extra words. Like a bonus track. For all its unplanned arrival in the world, it's one of my favorites. It's a story that started as a mad little phrase that got stuck in my head one day and became that wonderfully morose title. Funny how things can just knock on your door like that.

everyone you love will be eaten by wolves

I WAS fourteen when I realized I could see people die. Not everyone. Not at first.

I was visiting my grandma in the hospital, in one of her rarer moments of lucidity. I did not know she was "on her way out" as my dad put it. I was making as much small talk as I knew how to make when she suddenly sat up in bed, all wrapped in white and gray, and asked me how long she'd been there.

"Two weeks," I said.

"Two weeks?" She looked surprised and dismayed, like someone who had dropped a treasured photograph somewhere along the way.

She held my hand, and I felt strange and somehow grown up. And that's when I saw it, clear as anything. My grandma laid back in her hospital bed, her toothless mouth quivering as she took in a shuddering breath, her eyes mercifully closed. There was a sound of a machine letting out a long bleep, near and intense. There was the figure of my father sitting at her side, his weathered face unreadable.

At first I thought nothing of it. Sudden fits of the imagination were not uncommon to me, and though the vision had been forceful and authentic, as though I had been temporarily displaced to another time and place, I did not dwell on it.

She had another two comfortable months before she let go. I was not there when she died.

The second time I saw a death was at her funeral, when my father held me close in ways that he never would outside of those everyday tragedies. I saw him, much older, mirroring his mother almost to a tee, as though time had robbed him of gender. He lay in much the same bed, took much the same last breath, and died much the same death. Only I was there at his side this time. A much older me. A man of forty, at least.

Me, the man of forty or so, held my dead dad's hand and said, "This is the best-case scenario."

For whatever reason, the visions did not worry me. Maybe I assumed I was still merely a victim of my own imagination—an imagination morbidly focused by my sudden introduction to mortality. Maybe I just accepted it in the same faintly astounded way I accepted the hair beginning on my navel, or the harsh, hot dreams that left me sticky and guilty in the night.

But as I shook hands with relatives and well-wishers, the process repeated. Not for everyone, not all the time. They were all grownups, and there was a uniformity to their demise that I guess was comforting. Nothing sudden or shocking. Most of them drugged and barely there. Going quietly into the night.

There was one, Carl, an older cousin who I did not know well, who I saw crumpled in a night-time alleyway, his huddled dark form surrounded by pools of pink as neon reflected on wet concrete. I saw a larger man, some skinhead in a leather jacket, landing kick after meaty kick to Carl's head, even as his friends were running, shouting at him to "Leave it, man! Leave it! Let's go!"

They thought I was crying because that's what young boys do at funerals.

Carl would not die for another two years, but I did not have to wait that long to find out if I was right. I knew that these were visions, not dreams. I don't know how I knew, but I knew.

It sounds perverse now to say that I found this development exciting, but I don't blame myself. I was young, and what kid didn't want superpowers? I pictured myself saving people, almost always girls, warning them of some terrible tragedy that was going to befall them, or better still being there to stop it. I never did that, though, and I'll tell you why. I'll get there in a moment, because this isn't really about me and what I can do, but I need you to see where I'm coming from.

It turned out finding excuses to touch people in school was harder than I'd thought. I'd try clapping a friend on the shoulder, but I quickly worked out that for whatever reason it was only skin on skin contact that made the visions work. It was autumn, so everyone was in long sleeves, and I could hardly just start touching people's hands, not without them thinking I was some kind of freak.

Opportunity came at Phys Ed. We were playing basketball, and Eddie Gray was marking me. He kept a hand reached out to me, as though ready to push me away at any moment. All I had to do was lean in and let his hand brush my arm. Nothing happened. For whatever reason, the visions, this strange talent, only worked now and then. There seemed to be no pattern to its success, at least none I could see.

I tried again in the changing rooms, this time just waiting until my buddy Ralph Weidman took his shirt off and socking him in the arm. Nothing happened, and he socked me back, but that was all par for the course.

The next vision happened quite by accident. As we were all heading back to class, crammed into a corridor, my hand brushed against that of a girl I did not know well, Nicola something. The vision came, as powerfully as ever, but I was not prepared for the brutality of it. The woman was Nicola, but it took me a while to realize it was. She was much older, maybe fifty, and she'd gained a lot of weight over the years. She was running through a forest, running as best she could, breath heaving while she favored a limp in her left leg. The forest was dark, but shot through with silver. And there was a noise, a noise like nothing I'd heard before, as though the very earth itself was moaning. Nicola ran, stumbled and fell, and then a pack of wolves was on her.

Wolves. It took me a dazed moment to realize what was happening, but they were wolves all right. Streaks of fang and fur, hollering at the backs of their throats as their jaws snapped like machines.

They came as though summoned from the shadows and descended on Nicola like a storm—snarling and barking and snapping and tearing. Nicola's screams were lost under the onslaught as she rolled and flailed ineffectually. It only ended when a sudden gush of crimson drenched the muzzle of the leader of the pack. The wolves did not slow to eat or worry their kill; as soon as Nicola stopped moving, they darted away, howling into the night.

I spent the rest of that day with my scalp fizzing, too stunned to talk or to listen. I got home, went to my room, and lay shivering under the covers until dinner was called.

I tried not to touch anybody for a while after that, but then one day my mother, out of nowhere, planted a kiss on my cheek. It was something she hadn't done since I'd entered my awkward adolescence, but she did it then. Maybe she'd seen the worry in my eyes, or maybe she meant nothing by it at all. I saw her death. It was ordinary. Blessedly ordinary. Terrible, and tragic, but usual.

It was kind of a relief, to be honest.

The next day Mandy Price put her hand on my neck as part of some game, and I saw her being torn to shreds by wolves. She wasn't in a forest; she was in a house. Her home, presumably. She was laying on a living room carpet, her legs braced against a door that was rocking and splitting under the thumping of an unseen snarling force. That sound, the sound like a mountain screaming, filled every inch of the world, drowning out Mandy's shouts, drowning out the breaking of glass as wolves flooded through a nearby window and began eating her alive.

The panic set in again. I had to be crazy. How could two girls, two women, die in the same way? The same obscene and incredible set of circumstances? Why were these visions so bafflingly, horrifyingly different to the ordinary tragedies of my parent's deaths?

That day I tried, and tried again. Craig Jenkins, Damian White, Ahmed Sing. All of them eaten by wolves. The last, Ahmed, his future self thin and balding and dressed in an expensive suit, stood atop an office building roof and stared in mute terror as the emergency door broke in, and the wolves burst out. He ran for the ledge, but did not get there in time.

That night I called on my friends. We brought a bottle of cider and went to the park and I got drunk for the first time and I told them. I told them, "The wolves are coming for us. The wolves are coming for all of us."

They did not understand, or did not want to.

I had to do something. Something to prove to myself I wasn't crazy. Something to stop what was coming. I had to figure out what it all meant.

It took me months to recognize the pattern. By that time, I was a little older, and able to take a part time job at the local CostSave. I worked my way onto the cashier, a perfect way to brush hands with a wide variety of passing strangers. It was then I noticed. Almost every one that was a few years older than me had what I had come to think of as regular deaths. Either car accidents or illnesses. But people my own age and younger, all of them were torn apart by wolves. Eaten alive. Some of them in strange places. One in an unfamiliar city. One on the slopes of a ski resort. But most of them right here in town, sometimes near places that were shockingly familiar.

One time I touched the hand of an eight-year-old boy as he traded his loose change for a candy bar. There he was, in his...late twenties? Early thirties...? Facing the wolves. The boy, now a man, sat in a dainty conservatory, a China cup held delicately between his fingers. He stared wide eyed at a moon that dominated the sky, while all around him the glass began to crack under the pushing maws and scraping paws.

So it was coming. They were coming. I knew I had years, decades, but that didn't seem much of a comfort. Not then. I had to know if there was an escape. Surely this apocalypse, this plague of wolves, whatever it was and whatever caused it, surely it could not engulf the world? A vacation, the last I would take with my parents, put paid to that notion.

A thousand miles away and more, I brushed fingers with a pretty server on a beachside bar on the Florida Keys. Then I watched her blood stain the midnight sand as her perfect neck was ripped open. There was no escape. Whatever this strange and terrible fate was, it waited for all of us, myself included.

In the next few years drinking myself incoherent became first my hobby, then my second job, and then my career. I would haunt the bars and clubs, grateful for the anonymity of crowds, the silence of loud music. I would look at each and every face, as they laughed and danced, and think: *Don't you know? Man, don't you know? Everyone you love will be eaten by wolves. Don't you know?*

Being with women was difficult. My first time was to a slightly older girl in an alleyway. I kept my face to the brick of the wall as she pumped her hips beneath me, her nails digging into the meat of my hip as she growled, "Come on, come, come on." In my head, I saw her hanging from a ladder of a fire escape, face set in utter shock as her knuckles turned white and her legs were stripped to bone beneath her.

I tried to find girls that the visions didn't come for, but realized by now that they came for everyone. Perhaps the talent matured with me, or maybe I just got better with practice, but now there was not a single soul I could not see the end of. As I got older and the elderly succumbed to their everyday deaths, I saw more and more wolves.

The woman I settled down with was the one that stuck around, and with some patience and understanding we helped each other up, finding jobs, renting a home, buying a car. We never talked about children, and for that I was grateful.

It was possible to forget about it, after a time, even though that every now and then when I touched my partner's hand, I'd see her awful screaming and note with some sadness that I was nowhere to be seen in her last moments. But it was possible to forget, to watch television, cook food, make love, and not think about it. I toned down my drinking, but every now and then I would get tanked up and go outside of nights to stand on my lawn and stare up at the moon, waiting. Sometimes when I did this, I would open my eyes as wide as they could, and stretch out my jaw, lolling my tongue in the cool night air. I would pant until I became dizzy. Waiting.

Years went by. My mother died, and I was there to say goodbye. My father died, and I was there to tell him that this, this death, was the best-case scenario. I remembered the visions, when this older me had seemed impossible to the child I once was. I knew there was not much time before the wolves came.

My partner would sometimes ask me what I was thinking about, in the dark, when I was supposed to be asleep. I did not have the heart to tell her that she, and everyone she loved, would be eaten by wolves.

I took more and more to standing on my lawn at nights

staring up at the moon. Panting, waiting. And I noticed I was not alone on my dim and ordinary streets. Others began to appear, lit dully by their porch lights. Some smoking cigarettes, some drinking straight from the bottle. All of us looking up at the moon.

I can't remember when I started hearing of the reports. I think it was on Facebook. Something about a supermoon, some astronomical rarity, but the first time I saw it, I knew with dread certainty that they were coming. I thought about telling people, people I loved, but decided on mercy. Others knew, though. I could see it in their face, across supermarket checkouts, waiting at the deli. I would catch someone's eye and see that doomed absolution. They knew.

Now I stand upon my lawn and stare up at the impossible, beautiful, terrible moon. It's so large it seems to push me down with its mass, push me down to my hands and knees. I stretch my eyes as wide as they can open, and I push out my tongue as far as it can go.

I see the other few on my street, my nightly companions. All of them low to the ground, some of them already clawing at their clothes.

Everyone you love will be eaten by wolves.

all of this happened

I've said before, I rarely write outside of fantasy, but this next one is perhaps the realist story I've ever written, in a very practical sense. It is, of course, a ghost story.

all of this happened

HE PUT another log in the log burner and carefully closed the hatch. The light through the little window flared cozily. She waited for him on the chaise lounge under the blanket they had brought down from the bedroom. She smiled. It was a good smile. A smile to remember, for sure.

"Are you ready?" she said.

"Almost."

He went to the cramped kitchen and poured two glasses of wine. The bottle had come free with the rental and seemed a little classier than the bottle he had bought with him from home. He sipped it from one of the tall glasses. It was good. It would be drank, and they would be tipsy, and warm, and romantic.

He stood a while, trying to memorize the moment. The sharp smell of the wine. The dust on the stone walls. The night pressing against the window like a separated lover.

"All of this happened," he said, alone in the kitchen.

"Are you ready?"

"Coming."

He handed her a glass and slid under the blanket. She put her head on his shoulder, and for a while he thought they should just stay like that, saying nothing, just smelling the faint aroma of her shampoo and feeling the rise and fall of each other's breathing. Eventually, she spoke.

"The app didn't download."

Well, she'd wanted to stay somewhere historical, and cozy, and good wi-fi hadn't been a pressing requirement. Solitude and ancient stone had been, and he'd found it in a converted gatehouse to an estate long since torn down, the immaculate grounds empty and spare this close to winter. It was the best he could afford. It was lonely, in that good way that makes you feel close and connected. He knew she loved it, and that made him glad.

And it was, of course, the perfect setting for a ghost story.

"I was really looking forward to that," she said, snapping him away from his thoughts. Her bottom lip booped out just enough to let him know sulking was an option. It made him laugh.

"So tell me one you remember," he offered.

"I don't remember any!"

"So make one up!"

She nudged him, rocking her whole body against his enough to nearly slosh his wine on the antique furniture. "You're the writer." she said, accusingly.

"I don't write ghost stories."

"But you make stuff up all the time. Tell me a ghost story."

He cleared his throat and set down his glass on the coffee table. In truth, he did have a story. He'd been building it in his head since she mentioned over dinner that it'd be fun to read each other scary stories that night. He had a story, and what's more, it was true. Mostly true. And he reckoned he could tell it, too. Tell it properly. That was important. Not everyone could do that.

"I do have a story, actually," he said, letting his eyes rest on the slowly ticking mantel clock. "About something that happened to me."

She shuffled closer to him, big eyes narrowing in skepticism. "Really?"

"Well, it's not really a story about ghosts. It's mainly a story about coincidences."

The clock ticked. The night waited, quietly.

"Go on, then," she said.

"Did I ever tell you I had a doppelganger?"

"No!"

He loved how theatrical she could be. She reminded him of some character from a silent movie, expressions all wide and exaggerated. He enjoyed it, and he put it away where he hoped he would remember it.

"Yeah, three actually," he said. "I had one at my old job, and one in uni. I never saw those ones though."

"Then how did you know you had a doppelganger?"

"People would tell me. At work, when I used to smoke, people would start talking to me about things I never even talked to them about. Then people would tell me they saw me out in the smoking area long after I'd quit. I never met the guy, but apparently he was the spit of me."

"Really?"

"Yeah. Same in Uni. Total strangers would come up to me and start talking like we'd already met. It was bizarre."

"Sounds it."

He took another sip of his wine before returning it to the table. "But I did meet one doppelganger, back when I was a kid. Maybe eight or nine years old. You remember I told you I went to that private school?"

She put a finger to her lip. "Like Hogwarts but with child abuse instead of magic?" She quoted me, gruffly.

"Yeah," he snorted a quick laugh and then grinned sheepishly at her recriminating stare. "I shouldn't joke about that," he conceded. "And this isn't anything like that. That's not my story, but it kind of matters. I'll explain. I'm getting ahead of myself."

"You were talking about your doppelganger."

"Nicholas Findley," I said, nodding.

"That's a made-up name," she scoffed.

"No, seriously, that was his name! Nicholas Findley, and he was the only doppelganger I ever met. We were in the same year, and some of the same classes. Everybody thought we looked alike."

"Handsome kid, then." She grinned.

He shook his head slowly. "We weren't really that alike. You know when people have similar features, but one of them's just a bit... you know... put together a bit odd?"

She laughed, covering her mouth as though embarrassed she might be caught. "Don't!" she said.

"I'm not kidding! He was like the luckier version of me. I was quiet and withdrawn, and he was popular and outgoing. Everyone liked him. No one was mean about it, but they'd point out that we looked alike. He was a good sport about it. He didn't have to be, I suppose."

"So, you weren't identical then?"

"We were identical enough that we had this plan. You know the old school photos, right? Where they managed to get a whole group, a hundred kids or so, in the same photo? Panoramic?"

"Yes."

"Well, this was before digital, and the school was old-fashioned even then, so the way they did it was, right, they had this camera that moved manually, swiveled on its head, and took photos as it went along."

"Okay, I follow you."

"So, if you were fast enough, and you didn't get caught,

you could start at one end of the photo, and run to the other end and..."

"Appear in the photo twice, yes. So?"

"So, that was the plan! Nicholas and I stand on opposite sides of the group, I'd step down from the bench we stood on and he'd appear in the photo twice. No one would get in trouble because we looked alike anyway."

"Sounds a bit mean."

"I think I was too young and stupid to take it personally. It was just a fun trick, and then there's...well." He picked up his wine glass and stared into it for a while. Then he looked at her. "You know how I told you all that stuff that went on at that school?"

"Yes." Her smile faded.

"None of that happened to me or anyone I knew, but... things like that have a way of...permeating a place, I suppose. Of getting in the group consciousness. We never understood what was happening, but there were...campfire stories, I guess. Ghost stories. And it made it seem like things weren't quite real, you know? Like the school was this..." He searched for a good word, wishing he'd had more time to prepare. A word that was evocative but still sounded natural. "...it was this *other* place, you know? Maybe it's the same for all kids, but going to that school felt like you were in a different world, with different rules. And that's going to matter in a little while, so keep that in mind, please."

She nodded. Serious now.

"I told you this was a story about coincidences, and it is. The other thing Nicholas and I had in common, is that summer we were both in car accidents."

He pointed to the scar on his head, the inches-long indentation that had been slowly revealed over the years as he'd lost his hair. Recalling being hit by a car was never a problem for him. The smell of hot rubber. The sight of the blood on his neighbor's yellow checked shirt. The controlled panic in his dad's voice as he'd spoken words of reassurance. The sound the needle made when it went into his head. It was funny how memory worked. He never had to carefully store that one away. It sat out in the open like a dropped vase.

He felt her hand grip his. "Oh god, he didn't die, did he?" she gasped.

He quietly cursed himself for dropping momentum and then nodded. "He wasn't as lucky as me. I got hit by a car, but he was in a crash and wasn't wearing a seat belt, so his parents lived but..." He looked at her, her rounded eyes and parted lips, and decided to spare the detail he'd carefully prepared. The images of broken glass and white running shoes scattered on a dark road were consigned to the cutting room floor. "Yeah, he died."

"Oh no, that's horrid!" she said. He liked that she unironically said things like "horrid." He wondered if he should stop telling the tale. She looked a little upset, and he didn't want to upset her. But he did want her to think he was clever, and talented, and interesting. And she *had* insisted on a ghost story, after all. He pressed on.

"So, when we got back to school from break, Nicholas didn't return. Our form tutor told us what had happened. I know it sounds awful, but I remember being a little put out. I had this stupid bandage around my head that I probably could have taken off, but I wanted people to know I'd been hit by a car and...childish, I know. Jealous of the guy even after something so awful. But let me go on. Because, it's like I said—maybe it's true of all kids, or maybe it was just that place, but it didn't take us long to...mythologize it. Him. Nicholas became a campfire story, and I think once you make someone a campfire story, it's easier to do what we did."

"What did you do?" She wasn't smiling at all now.

"We decided to go ahead with the photo trick..."

Her hand flew to her mouth. "Oh my god, that's awful! Surely not?"

Part of him was perversely delighted he had strung her along so well. Part of him wanted to stop and tell her that none of this was true, that this was the story she had wanted, and they were nearing the end, and it was all okay.

"Yeah. I would appear in Nicholas's place." He nodded. "Maybe we kind of wanted to immortalize him. Keep him going. Or maybe we just thought it was a fun trick. Maybe we just wanted our own ghost story. Probably that."

"That's terrible!"

"Let me finish," he said.

"You didn't let them make you do it, did you?"

"Darling, I was a lonely boy. I didn't have many friends, and all of a sudden, I was the hero of the hour. Of course I agreed to do it! I didn't take much convincing at all. I'm not proud of it, but I was just a kid…"

"But his parents! His poor parents…"

"I know, but it doesn't matter anyway. I chickened out."

"You did?"

He finished the wine, letting it sit on his tongue a while before swallowing. "Yeah, I did. Not because I thought of the consequences or anything like that. There was this teacher, Mr. Jones—took us for rugby—and he was a scary looking guy. Glass eye that never seemed to blink. I don't know if someone tipped him off or if I was just paranoid, but he seemed to be looking at me throughout the whole set up. Like he knew I was going to try something. I chickened out. I didn't run for the other side."

She nodded. The clock ticked. The night was silent. "Good," she said. "I'm glad."

"I still got in trouble, though," he said, quietly.

"Why?"

"Because if you ever look at that photo, you'll see me on

the left-hand side of it..." He paused for dramatic effect. "...and someone who looks just like me on the right."

For a while she said nothing, then she pushed him, shaking her head.

He laughed. "What?"

"You really had me going there."

"You said you wanted a ghost story!"

"Yeah, but not stories about little boys who died!"

"I made that part up. No one died."

"I *knew* Nicholas Findley was a fake name."

"No, that was a real boy in my class. He wasn't my doppelganger, though. I had a Uni doppelganger and a work doppelganger but never a school one. I should have used Richard Mason; he had a nice believable name. Not a nice kid, though."

"So, none of it was true?"

"Well, I definitely got hit by a car. And there *was* a way to trick school photographs, a couple of kids tried it, but it never worked. We had the photos taken on a gravel drive, you see, so they'd hear you if you ran. The ghost part was lifted from a story I used to read as a kid, though. I wish I could tell you the name, it was a good one."

She snuggled into him again. He laughed.

"I didn't like that!" she said, accusingly.

"It was supposed to be spooky!"

"Yeah, but I'm freaked out now!"

"Just as well that story app didn't download then," he said. Then he put his arm around her. "Aw, you poor thing."

The clock ticked. The night remained.

"You shouldn't do that, you know," she whispered.

"What?"

"You shouldn't salvage real things for fiction. It doesn't feel right. Not when it's real."

The fire began to fade and the room darkened, his eyes grew heavy. "All of this happened."

"What?" Her head lifted from the nook of his neck, jerking him from his doze.

"Nothing," he said. "Just something I say to help me remember moments."

"Does it work?"

He shrugged. "I don't know what I don't remember. It happened or it didn't. It's like taking a photo that you put away in a shoebox. If you forget, then it didn't happen until you open the box."

"Schrodinger's memory," she said, smugly.

The room became colder. The night became the distant, unremarkable thing it always was.

"Yeah." His eyes grew heavy again, so he closed them, and smiled sleepily. "Schrodinger's ghosts."

"That's silly. Don't speak now."

"It's true, I think. You, me. We're all ghost stories eventually. Just things we remember and things we tell each other."

"Don't say that."

"It's true, though," he said. "All of this happened."

star breaker

If we've learned anything about me so far, dear reader, it is that I am not above taking dreams and strange mental fixations as basis and motivation to get something on the page. Perhaps this is normal, I don't know. I mention it now because this next one is a mix of both—a brief, contextless, and horrifying scene that came to me in my sleep, and an eighties metal song that I simply could not snap out of my brain for weeks. If you can guess the song, just imagine it playing continuously. Endlessly. Whether you want it to or not. Enjoy!

star breaker

RETRO KEPT his eyes front and fixed on the forward monitor. The heavy metal music blared through his earbuds, drowning out the eternal hum of the life support system. He sat, as he mostly always sat, in the pilot's chair. Not that he would, or even could, do much piloting. Retro was half-convinced he was only even there so ground control could cite human error if something went wrong. There wasn't much to bump into between Earth and Mars.

An electric guitar whined loudly, and Retro grinned ear to ear, a grin with a lot of pressure, like he might suddenly crush his teeth into diamonds. In his wraparound sunglasses, the reflection of the looming red planet hung impassively. Waiting there on the monitor screen, it looked just like its pictures. It was strange. He knew it was inhospitable, that the atmosphere would choke him in seconds and the temperature would freeze him to death in minutes, but hanging out there in the black the planet seemed the warmest, most inviting thing he'd seen in forever.

It had been months aboard *Star Breaker*. Months of tube food and vitaboosters. Months of omni-gym and vacuum toilets. Months of media re-runs. Months of checking stats and course corrections he didn't really need to check and could likely do nothing about. Retro wasn't really here for the craft; he was here for the cargo.

The cargo. He felt a shudder run down his back despite the always comfortable memogel padding of the pilot chair. The weird fear was something he never talked about in his daily wellness checks. He knew it was irrational, so there was no need to rationalize it. Lying to therapists was something he'd mastered when he was just a teenager. There was no real trick to it—you figured out what you were supposed to say and you said it.

His perfect mental health record was one of the reasons he'd been shortlisted for Operation Kaleidoscope. Twelve months alone in space (*technically alone*, he thought, and shuddered) was a tall ask for anyone, but Elite Horizon had some very specific and powerful backers with some very specific requests. A human had to be on board. An ordained Humanist minister, to boot. Retro checked all the boxes. Flight experience. A stint on the International Space Station. Passably spiritual and mentally robust. Not too far from retirement and somewhat disliked by his colleagues. All the boxes.

There had been talk of sending two people on the mission, but the consensus had been that would only have doubled the potential for human problems. Also, it would have doubled the staffing costs. Even Elite Horizon, backed as it was by some of Earth's most obscenely wealthy clientele, had margins to consider. Retro didn't care either way. It was a lot of money to babysit a simple mission. He was nearly at the drop zone. Soon he would be done, and then just six more months until he was on a beach somewhere.

Yeah. A beach. Blue seas. Blue skies. Hot sand. Hot cocktail waitresses. A guy could see out his last days in style on what he'd take home from this gig. It was not like he had anyone to pass it onto. A cavalcade of nearly wives, a sister he hadn't seen in decades, parents long dead. No kids, obviously. He'd never really thought about kids as anything but something that happened to other people. All in all, it was a simple plan, and so a good one. A reassuring one. Cocktails and then death. No need to think about the gray areas between.

The mission was pure cake, but still he couldn't shake the dream. Even as he thought about it, he flicked his gaze nervously over his shoulder. The bulkhead doors remained closed, as they had been since takeoff. They opened in the dream though, and he stepped into the airlock and then on to the cargo freight...

Retro pressed the Volume Up icon on his media player. It was already at max. A high-pitched voice wailed about gliding through the sky. He fixed his gaze on Mars, getting a little bigger every second, it seemed.

"Soon, baby," he said, and made himself jump. His voice was croaky. It didn't sound like him at all. He wondered how long it had been since he'd spoken. His daily wellness check, for sure. But when was that? He didn't even remember what they talked about. Did they talk? Had he somehow skipped it? If so, for how long?

Sleep was different in space. They tried to manage the circadian rhythms with NIR and UV lighting as much as possible, but still the dreams were vivid. Worse than their intensity was their lack of variety. There were only ever two dreams. Sometimes he dreamed he was in this chair, and nothing was different, and he woke up wondering if he'd ever slept at all. Other times he dreamed of going through the bulkhead doors. A dream or a nightmare, it depended on how long he thought about it. He tried not to think about it.

Was he sleeping now?

The comm panel beeped, shaking him out of whatever he had been in. He cleared his throat and hit the receive icon, only just remembering to remove his earbuds and sunglasses.

"Hello!" he said. His voice was still scratchy. "Hello." He tried again. Better.

Lucy's face, freckled and sun-damaged, filled the screen. Her smile quickly turned to a frown of concern. "Jesus, Tom, you look like shit. You need to get yourself ready before drop. People are going to be watching this."

Retro lifted his fingers self-consciously to the rough beard growth on his face. "You didn't seem to mind yesterday..."

Lucy frowned. "Yesterday? Tom, we moved our check-ins from daily to weekly a month ago. Remember?"

Retro thought. He didn't remember. Not really. "Yes, of course. Sorry."

"Did you just wake up?"

Retro assumed that, reasonably, he might have. Who could tell? "Yes, I did. I must have overslept."

Lucy nodded, well-practiced sympathy returning to her face. "Well, you're running late, but you still have time. Remember, the camera feed is pumping this out live. We need you looking your best. You're the face of Elite Horizon today. I trust you have the speech memorized by now?"

Retro forced out a little laugh. "It's been six months and I've had little else to do," he said. He was lying, though. The truth was he hadn't looked at the speech. Not even once. He didn't really know why that was. It was one of the few things they'd asked him to do. He supposed in a pinch he could just read it from his palmtop. "You don't need to worry about it," he lied again.

"Okay." She stared at him a second too long. "I'll check back in at oh nine hundred ship time. You'll be together by then?"

"Absolutely."

"Out." Lucy's image faded to the comm system's ready screen. Retro stared for a while at the artfully ascending white line on blue that was Elite Horizon's logo.

It made him think of the dream. The dream where he heard the voices behind him. The dream where he rose slowly, unstoppably, from the pilot's chair and activated the bulkhead door. In the dream he was always frightened. He didn't want to go through the bulkhead door. He didn't want to stand in the airlock as it opened onto the cargo hold. The fear he felt wasn't even rational. The *rational* fear would be that the cargo area had no life support. It didn't need any. He'd be dead in seconds. The other fear, the other *rational* fear, was that even wearing his E-suit he might mess up the unloading sequence and that he, along with the *Star Breaker*'s payload, would drift helplessly out into the unknowable void, there to spin endlessly into nothing.

Those were completely rational fears. Unlikely, but rational.

The cargo. The cargo itself. That was the irrational fear.

In the dream, he walked into the hexagonal metal cavern hearing nothing but reverent silence, like a cathedral to an absent god. The emergency lights snapped on one by one until they reached the end of the long, metal corridor, and picked out in their red glow he saw the thousand metal sarcophagi, each with a portal window. Behind each portal, a gray face, wide-eyed and smiling. In the dream he walked the length of the corridor, the lights snapping off behind him, until he was alone in the dark but for a thousand pairs of eyes, glinting. Then he would hear the whispering of a thousand dry voices.

"Take my hand. Where we go, none have been. We seed the future. We are the future. Burn with us. Take my hand."

Retro shuddered again and placed the earbuds firmly into his ears. The guitars resumed and a wailing voice told him that paradise was waiting, but only for a chosen few. He looked over to his environment suit, standing ready on the wall. Some time ago he'd placed googly eyes on the plastech dome of the helmet. He supposed he'd have to take them off before the drop. People would think he was crazy. Rich and important people. And it wasn't long until the drop. Not long at all.

He stood up and stretched and thought about his speech. What would he say? Oh, he had an idea about what Elite Horizon wanted him to say, but what would he say? That the bodies of a thousand yuppies, carefully refrigerated, would soon be dropped over the skies of Mars, there to burn, and smash into the red dust, and give to the soil the nourishing ashes of their flesh and the canny bacteria of their guts. That they would become the sustenance and earth of a new world, in a small but meaningful way. The foundational wave of Mars' careful terraforming. Would he mention that the ludicrous price-tag they paid for this honor would fund dozens of missions yet to come? Did he need to justify it? Cheapen it?

He thought of the falling bodies, glittering in the atmosphere like cosmic sperm, seed spilled on fertile ground. The thought made him grin that high-pressure grin again.

He hadn't realized, in his musing, that he'd been slowly climbing into the E-suit, making sure his media player was tucked safely inside. He placed the helmet over his head, and the sudden compression drove the earbuds further in. The hard rock music filled every inch of this new, closer reality. He noticed he left the googly eyes on the helmet's visor, but he didn't care. This wasn't really about the people watching. It wasn't even about the rich bodies. This was just primal instinct writ large. Him. The corpses. Ground control. All cells of the same siphonophores organisms.

Before he knew it, the bulkhead door was closing behind him. The comms light on his HUD was blinking, but he ignored it. A wailing voice was telling him to take his hand, and to understand. The airlock door opened onto the cargo hold, revealing the rows and rows of refrigerated coffins. It was the work of a moment to authorize the manual override on the locking controls, and soon each and every coffin hissed open.

In the low gravity the coolant particles hung like party smoke, and one by one the corpses bumped out into the open, a bumbling waltz of pale-skinned cadavers.

To think he'd been afraid. He set in the sequence to open the cargo bay door. An orange beacon began to flash rhythmically, making the bodies seem vital, almost like they were moving of their own accord. Smiling, Retro pushed off the ground and joined them. Soon he was floating in a vortex of elegantly swirling bodies, bumping gently against one another in a passionless orgy. He saw breasts and genitals, fat bodies and thin, afros and braids, all made uniform gray by death and cold. And so many staring eyes. Were all the bodies all smiling? He thought they were.

The room brightened as the cargo bay door opened, revealing the red planet beneath them. The whole congregation began to float lazily toward the exit, as though some unseen hand had rung a dinner bell.

Retro laughed. This was it. This was destiny. No rotting away for him. No brutal callousness of old age and decrepitude. No watching himself die by years and months and weeks, corrupted and dehumanized and artificially postponed by medical poisons and limited miracles. Not for him the gray areas between cocktails and death. This was the way to go. Not to end, but to begin something new.

Drums pounded and the guitars picked out a steady, unstoppable rhythm. Retro surrendered his body to the powerful pull of planet and destiny.

fresh new hell

Here's the thing about comedy, and fiction as we know it. It's doomed. Thanks to social media I can tell a joke that implies an entire fiction concept in a single tweet and people will consume it, forget about it, and then move onto the next like some kind of relentless, tubby, caterpillar bastard. That's what this next story started as—an easily digestible couple of sentences that briefly filled a gap in the whirling kaleidoscope of passive media consumption. What possible reason could there be to expand it into a short story? Anyway, here is that short story.

fresh new hell

THE BEAST WAITED as it had waited years beyond counting. Years beyond knowing. Chained in void and choked in darkness, it knew only the hungry anticipation of return, and the memory of sweet and gruesome victories.

Ashk'nte—feeder of foolishness, devourer of hope, bane of man.

To be a demon was to be at the beck and call of man, both their salvation and their punishment. A simple arrangement, really. To be brought forth before those drunk on their imagined power, on their borrowed magiks and unearthed secrets, to be bound and commanded and to wait, patiently, for the slightest crack in their control. And then to pounce. And then to visit upon them in punishment, terrible ironies and vicious tortures, to soak their souls in deepest regret, and weave them through with unbearable new heartache.

Nourishment. Food.

Ashk'nte could be patient. It had been. With sometimes months between its earthbound visits and sometimes years. It had no way to pass the time but for the passing faces of man. The first, so long ago, a squat and hirsute being, barely uncrouched from a creature, happening by chance against the impacted runes at the bottom of the cave, his fingers tracing them in ignorance.

The cave dweller's wishes had been simple—no more than a desire for cooked meat and warmth. Ashk'nte had set the man on fire. Simple.

And many of its first encounters were like that, simple humans, stumbling upon the summoning words by folly or by farce, with no comprehension of the powers they meddled with. It met them in the forests, in the caverns, in the stone circles and midnight huts. And each time it gave them what they craved and found a way to make it their destruction.

Perhaps it was unfair. After all, it had been made whole from stars and darkness, while the humans had barely shivered off the dank mud of their own less dignified creation. Ashk'nte was not here to be fair. It was here to test, and to punish. That was its purpose. That was its fierce desire.

And punish it had, throughout the ages of man. As that low and naked beast had become more upright, he had become more arrogant, no longer a shivering bag of bones huddled around his bonfires. Now came kings and wisemen, adorned in oil and gold with painted faces and imperious smirks. They came from their cities and their palaces to challenge the demon, to try and harness its power. They came with mages and wizards, some with skill and some merely charlatans. And one by one Ashk'nte humbled them all.

Ashk'nte recalled fondly a king of mighty intellect, who had asked him, foolishly, for all the knowledge of the world. The demon had filled his tiny mind with so much of his own cosmic insignificance that the king had gone quite quickly mad and dashed his cultured brains out on the pavement beneath his balcony. Ashk'nte recalled a thin and bright-eyed queen, who had demanded her beauty be made eternal. He'd turned her flesh to marble, and she stood to this day gathering dust in a mausoleum somewhere. Ashk'nte recalled so many, many happy days.

It was difficult to measure the progress of human ages, trapped as the demon was in lingering slumber throughout the passing years. It gleaned what it could from the changing faces and technologies of those who discovered its summoning runes, as their stone tablets had evolved to scrolls and then to grimoires. There had been a time of great slowing, where its summoning became fewer and further between. The churches and cults of man had coalesced like water drops on a leaf, and unusual runes and rituals were outlawed in a time of fire and fear. It had slept for a long time, then, until gentler ages had once more stirred the dark curiosities of mortal minds.

Ashk'nte had next emerged to electric lights and concrete walls and men who had called themselves Germans. It had been impressed at the machines and contraptions of the time, but such technology did not guarantee mastery of the ancient ways. The German men had wished for power, and the demon had called down lightning, dooming their metal machines and giving them far more power than man's still frail body could absorb.

It wondered idly what surprises the next summoning would hold for it, and how it would turn those surprises to its advantage.

Its eyes, formless though they were, opened. In the empty peace of the netherrealm, the whisper of change may as well have been a scream. At last some hapless mortal sought to summon him again. The burning blue of the summoning ring appeared before Ashk'nte, festooned with runes that were as familiar to it as its own name and purpose. It felt its essence dragged unstoppably toward the ring. For all its power, the demon could not resist the pull of summoning nor banishment, this was Ashk'nte's only weakness.

It took form and grinned a long and jagged grin. Once it

had appeared as boars and bears and unimaginable dragons, but it had long since learned that man found no form more unsettling than that of another man. It drifted unstoppably, licking its blue lips in anticipation for whatever new age it would materialize in, and what humorous delights might await it there. There violent blue of the summoning ring became all encompassing, until the demon once more felt the faint pleasure of air, and dust and gravity. It stood and blinked.

"Aooooo shit! Whaddup internet, it's ya boi Captain Magic once again bringing you premium content and ho-lee-shit do I deliver or do I deliver? It's a genuine blue-assed demon, son, straight up. Standing there with its dick out like I did not just rip a hole through space and time. Rude! Moxy! I love it."

The demon blinked and tried to understand what it was seeing and hearing. The tongues of men were simple things, but although the demon understood each word that had been spoken, it was having difficulty deciphering exactly what was being said by the human. And the human itself was puzzling. It's dress, for example. Not the robes of kings, or the tough suits of the Germans, but not the rags of peasants either. It seemed to be swaddled in light, colorful fabrics, adorned with words and symbols the meaning of which eluded the demon's experience. And the devices... The dwelling was tiny, but reeked of power. Behind the smiling human were huge glowing tablets that fairly hummed with energy, displaying baffling reams of pictures and words. The human held another tablet in his hand, a palm sized slate of onyx that glowed as he brushed his fingers against it.

"What...?" the demon stuttered, uncertain for the first time in its long and patient existence.

The human spoke, but once again did not seem to be speaking to the demon. Rather he seemed to be talking to a glowing glass eye that perched atop one of the blinding tablets.

"I'm a wizard, baby, a genuine magic user, so y'all can just suck my wand. I wanna see wands in the chat, I wanna see demons in the chat. GenMan Fifty Nine, you own me a Coke, dude. The rest of you dweebs keep the supers coming in, put your money where your ass is, crackers!"

"What is this?" the demon demanded.

The human, Captain Magic, turned in his swiveling throne as though noticing the demon for the first time. "Oh, right, you're not from around here, are ya, bud?"

The demon drew in a breath and composed itself. "I am from the endless voids of—"

"Yeh yeh yeh yeh, I know it, dude, it was all in the manual. This..." The one called Captain Magic gestured to the glowing tablets. "This is the internet!"

The demon narrowed its eyes. "What is an internet?"

"Oh its like tubes n' shit." The human cackled wildly. "It's the fucking internet, dude! Like a gazillion computers all talking to each other. Say hi, we've got over a hundred thousand views on this stream, you're practically famous right now. Say hi, man!"

"How high?" the demon stammered uncertainly.

Captain Magic blinked a couple of times in puzzlement. "Oh yeah, that's right, you gotta do what I tell you!"

The demon's burgeoning fear subsided. Here was more familiar ground. Humanity had grown strange, certainly, but short-sighted greed was clearly still at their core. Ashk'nte would destroy this man as it had destroyed all the foolish pretenders before him.

"I command you to helicopter your dick!" the human said, smugly.

Ashk'nte felt the panic of confusion rise again. "I do not know what a helicopter is..."

The human made an impatient gesture. "Show the people what you got, dude!"

This was all wrong, Ashk'nte knew. It wondered if humanity had been replaced somehow, by some subtle new breed of demon. "How is it you came to summon me, mortal?" it demanded.

Captain Magic shrugged. "Found it on Reddit."

"What is a Reddit?"

Captain Magic laughed. "Aw, dude you are dumb as shit. This is awesome."

Ashk'nte tensed, balking at the crack it sensed in its millennia forged resolve, it's endless void-bred patience. It calmed itself and prepared to invite this human, this Captain Magic, to confide his fondest desires. The cunning words had barely reached his lips when there was a familiar sensation and a bright flash of blue. A new summoning ring had appeared.

Ashk'nte stared in shock. His exiting from the mortal realm almost always came with the destruction of the one who had called him. Only few times had he been banished; once by a crone, once by a fool, and once by a boy whose only wish was for Ashk'nte's freedom, for some reason. To see the summoning ring while still on the mortal plain was unprecedented. Horrifying in its incongruity.

"Oh, looks like time's up, dude. I guess someone else worked it out."

Ashk'nte gaped in bafflement. Was the secret of his power no longer so jealously guarded? "How many know the runes?" he demanded.

Captain Magic shrugged. "Dude, it's on the fucking internet. Everyone knows them."

Before it could comment or curse, Ashk'nte was drawn into the ring. It blinked in the strange new light, an eldritch pink and purple it had never seen before.

"Uwu demon daddy!" came a voice.

Ashk'nte blinked. What was this new demon? It had the body of a woman—abundantly accentuated by garments tighter than any shroud it had ever seen—but it had the ears and paws of a cat, even a tail coming from its... No, that could not be.

"I've been a bad little kitty!" It spoke. "Are you going to take me to hell and punish me?"

Ashk'nte stared. "What manner of succubus are you?"

The being turned to a bank of the now familiar magic tablets. Ashk'nte could see similar glyphs and images as those of Captain Magic's domain, but he noticed that many of the images where of the cat-beast itself, many different angles, but most focusing on—

"Is..." Ashk'nte swallowed. "Is that tail coming out of your anus?"

"Ooooo, such filthy talk, demon daddy! Maybe I should punish you!"

Ashk'nte stepped back just as another portal opened.

"Oh, too bad!" the cat-thing sang. "I had such sights to show you!"

The demon leaned gratefully toward its salvation, but no sooner had it done so than another portal opened. This was unheard of. Unthinkable. Two summoning rings at once? Ashk'nte screeched in pain and horror as it felt its essence being pulled in two different directions at once. With all of its might it pulled itself toward the nearest portal, scrambling through. It lay gasping on the floor and looked up—

"Ya done got Flabber Blasted, mother fucker!" someone screamed.

Ashk'nte screeched as two soft and colorful darts bounced off its head. It looked up into a face of a small child, its face alive with malignant glee. It held some sort of whirring wand in its hand, that suddenly popped, sending another of the soft darts at it. The child fell to the floor laughing, and behind it, sure enough, the terrible flickering eyes of the magic tablets.

Their impassive beaming of eternal nonsense, ceaseless, relentless, merciless.

"No," the demon moaned, shocked and humiliated to hear its voice so weak.

Another portal opened, but for the first time in its existence, Ashk'nte felt no anticipation. Not even relief. What dread awaited it? What fresh new awfulness? Its terror doubled as first one summoning ring appeared, and then another. This time it was not close enough to escape. It screeched in agony as its arm was pulled one way while the rest of its body was pulled the other.

"Ha! Flabber Blasted!" the child yelled, righteously. "Mother fucker!"

Ashk'nte came to shivering in yet another, small, comfortable, buzzing abode filled with cacophonous rhythms. It looked up into the glaring twin eyes of yet more magic tablets. "Please no," it mewled. "No more."

Yet another human wizard danced in front of Ashk'nte's crumpled, vulnerable form. It seemed to be gyrating its groin with uncanny speed.

"That's right!" the human screamed. "Uh-huh! Yeah! Now it's on, baybee! Wooo! THIS is how we helicopter."

The demon croaked but could not even plead for its life as first one summoning ring appeared, and then a second, a third.

It screeched as it fell into the nearest, leaving one of its feet behind in a shred and pop of agony. It did not even get to see the next hellish cell. A summoning ring was already waiting for it, and another.

"Subscribe to my channel—"

"Follow me for more—"

"Hey there, and welcome to—"

"SMASH THAT LIKE—"

Each time a piece was ripped from its flesh, Ashk'nte

thought that it would become accustomed to the torment. That the agony might fade. But it did not. As portal after portal appeared, and with each terrible pinching loss of its essence, flesh it had always supposed eternal and invincible, Ashk'nte comforted itself that it might know death.

The humans had defeated it. What had they become? These howling mages? These invincible jesters? These all-powerful morons? Avatars of their all-seeing electric god. Humanity had seized the powers of hell, surely, and they had not needed the likes of Ashk'nte to do so.

As each fresh scream ripped from its bloodied throat, Ashk'nte braced himself for nothingness. Yes, oblivion, true oblivion, was what it craved now. And surely there was nowhere else to go? It had been dragged through hell. Surely there was no lower place than this.

neutral

Okay, this next one is morose even for me. But, come on, who doesn't feel like this after a bit of doomscrolling? Or maybe I just need to get off the internet, man, I dunno. One day I might write my satirical thriller about a charismatic millennial serial killer who murders to offset his carbon footprint, but for now, there's this.

neutral

IT'S RAINING IN JULY, but that doesn't mean anything. The average human produces seven tons of carbon a year. Ten tons if you're a white, western, male, which I inescapably am. I'm thirty-two years old. That's three hundred and two tons of carbon, minimum, just because I exist. Probably more. It's like student loan debt: there forever, whether you really got anything out of it or not.

I sit in my car, watching the rain patter and tap against my windscreen like a gentle, distant riot. The car is an early two thousand model diesel. I bought diesel because at the time they told me it was more efficient and better for the environment. Turns out that wasn't true, and diesel exhaust particulates are a major contribution to air pollution. Sometimes the only thing that helps me sleep at night is that diesel particulates are also a contributing cause of lung and bladder cancer in humans.

Swings and roundabouts.

But, no, that's not right. That doesn't matter. Humans breed like rabbits and insist on living to become obscene, useless skeletons whose only function and contribution is to consume and to have consumed. To either die alone or else simper over their cherub cheeked replacements who will go on to consume and to have consumed. A few early deaths from diesel fume cancer is a drop in the acidic, dying ocean. I mean, we had a whole global pandemic and what did we do? We carried on like it was nothing. Shook it off. Millions dead and barely a scratch. It's awful when you think about it. We're unstoppable. There's nothing we can't beat. Not god, not nature, not ourselves.

It's times like this that any sensible man realizes there's only one thing he can do to make a difference.

I get out of the car, push the button to lock the door behind me, and drop the keys on the floor where they clatter next to a couple of dank cigarette butts.

I stand on the concrete promenade—an ugly, endless step built a century ago to stop the casual erosion of the waves. And protecting what? A shore lined with identi-kit caravans that cater to an army of dried-up and sexless retirees as they seek a brief purgatory of denial between useful life and care home dependency.

It is July, but the beach is gray and the distant ocean grayer still. That doesn't mean anything. The rain has already plastered my shirt to my skin. I take it off and feel the elements against my hairless, ape body. I want to feel, here and now, this one last time, like I am a part of the world. Something of it, and not despite it. That doesn't happen, though. Even as I kick off my shoes and socks and march across the sodden sand, I'm still just me. None of the tedious self-awareness departs as I commit myself to absolute and noble purpose. I am still aware that I did not take my laundry out of the dryer this morning. I am still cognizant that the woman I went for coffee with two weeks ago did not call me back as she said she would. I am still cold.

I am quietly optimistic that there's only one thing that can really free you from yourself.

The last thing I take off is my jeans, carefully ensuring my wallet and smartphone and my note are in the pockets. I want them to know I am gone. I do not want choppers and boats burning through fossil fuels to find my body. I want, in my last, nothing more than to feed the fish that I have fed on, and to leave it at that small restitution.

Now in my underwear I stride into the sea, the wind blasting white noise into my head. The shock from the cold is immediate, and the stony sands are hard on my feet. I am aware of every minor scratch and scrape and am ashamed of how loudly and selfishly each one vies for my attention. It's like every cell of my body is inherently entitled. It's disgusting, really, when you think about it.

The water is up to my knees now, and I gasp as a sudden wave briefly submerges my crotch. I think about diving in and speeding this up a little, but I suppose there's no rush.

I've fantasized about this for a while now. But not quite like this. In my dreams I'm not alone. In my dreams I am part of a chain stretching for all the many miles of Britain's coasts. All of us naked as babies, our black, brown, and definitely white skins bared fully to the world. We're united, man and woman, young and old. In my dreams we step forward together, arms linked, smiling defiantly as we return to the sea. Evolution come full circle.

But not everybody has my courage, or my resolve.

The water is up to my neck, and the smell of salt and brine fills my nose. Submerged, my body is numb and finally stops shaking. This beach has a bathing rating of "sufficient" according to the UK government website.

The water closes over my head, freezing my scalp. Beneath the water it is cloudy and obscured and mercifully, wonderfully quiet. Yes. This is it. This is how the world takes me back into it. Silent and dark as a womb. Even the cold will numb me completely soon, and then it will be warm. I will float and sleep as though I was never born. I will be forgiven as an innocent.

There's a pressure in my lungs, but I'm ready for it. I've read about this. Apparently, when you drown, there's a euphoria at the end. Some struggle and panic as my selfish body tries to maintain the status quo, but then a rushing peace as it accepts its place in the world. I'm here for it. I'm ready for that homecoming. I'm

The sea water hits the back of my nose and it burns. My arrogant, selfish body flails, fighting tooth and nail against my judgment. I put my feet down and stand up. I suppose at some point the waves must have rolled me backward because the water only comes to my knees again. I cough a splutter of brine and stand with my hands on my hips, breathing raggedly.

The air hits me and it's cold. Freezing. I'm shivering again now. I look out into the wide, oblivious sea. All I need to do is walk forward. Harder this time. Maybe swim out and keep swimming until I haven't got the strength left to swim anymore. I am suddenly so, so tired.

The heater blasts warm air into my face. I shake madly as I wait to dry off, lamenting that I did not pack a towel for this seventy-mile round trip. I put something mindless on the radio, but I'm not really listening to it over the comforting burble of the car's idling engine. I want to be angry. I want to weep. But all my traitor body feels is relief. And hunger. And comfort. As my late two thousand model diesel car puffs thousands of milligrams of particulate into the atmosphere of a seaside car park, I begin to doze off. Safe, warm, and hideously content.

bedtime

I remember being young and daydreaming about if and how I would survive the apocalypse. Looking back, I really should have been daydreaming about more useful things given that the world has not ended. Yet.

Now that I am older and slower, I have ceased to wonder how I would fare at the end of society. I'll leave that to the young and pretty, who can pull off a leather bikini more convincingly than I.

I wrote this next one when I was a new father and realized exactly how fragile happiness is.

bedtime

THERE WAS A NOISE. It was difficult to move quietly in the factory where, empty as it was, sound tended to bounce and carry along the flat concrete floors. The man considered it lucky he had chosen that time to take a piss, and reflected it was the first luck he had seen in a long while. He returned to his little camp behind the dusty machinery cautiously and saw the drifter nudging the empty sleeping bag with his foot. The man had left his oil lantern burning on a low light, and the drifter had come as a moth, skulking above the scraped-clean cooking pot before turning his attention to a mostly empty backpack, which he began to rifle through with rodent eagerness.

The man stepped from the shadows, the crowbar easy in his hand. The first time he tried to speak, he managed only a dry croak. He cleared his throat and tried again.

"Something I can help you with?"

The drifter sprang back, his eyes white and sudden on a face made black with grime. A knife was in his fingers with practiced liquidity.

"Oh, Jesus fuck, I thought you were one of them," the drifter said, his relief vying with his caution. His accent was local. The man wondered how long they had been hiding in the same area.

"I ain't," said the man. "Now go away."

The drifter's mouth opened and closed for a little while. "Come on, guy. I'm just hungry is all. There's no food out there, and you got food in that pack, I know it."

The man stepped forward and opened his long coat. He gestured down at the absence of his belly. "You see me gaining weight? You think I'm being greedy?"

The drifter's eyes flicked from the man's face to the crowbar in his hand. "I didn't want no trouble," he said.

The man nodded. "You and your knife not looking for trouble. And if I'd been asleep in that bag—would I have woke up, do you think?"

"Hey, fuck you," sneered the drifter. "I just want to eat, guy. Now you back the hell away from me." The drifter held his blade out threateningly and reached down to pick up the backpack. The man was quick, though—very quick for someone who'd eaten nothing but tinned soup for two weeks. The crowbar swung and glanced the side of the drifter's head, who grunted like a hog and collapsed to the ground. A quick flit of crimson erupted from the gash above his eye and steadied to a sticky flow on the concrete floor.

The man stood a while, waiting for his dizziness to subside. The drifter's breath was now coming in deep rumbling snores, and his eyes were rolling madly in his head. In a sudden flurry of busyness, the man reached down into his backpack and pulled out a roll of electrical tape. He bound the drifter's hands and feet together, and without a pause began to drag the semi-conscious body across the floor toward a dark windowed office area.

The drifter began to come around, trying to speak but succeeding only in making a hollow bellow. The man ignored him, breathing heavily through his nose as he fished a keyring from within his coat and began to fumble through it.

"Where am I?" said the drifter. "Alice? Mike? Oh god, Mike, look at his eyes—his eyes!"

The man ignored the babbling, found the key he was looking for, and opened the office door. Inside, the room was barely lit by another oil lamp. Devoid of furniture, the sparse concrete floor was thick with dust. A keen eye would have been able to make out a thin chalk line, stretching the length of the room. The man entered, dragging the drifter along with him.

"What's that smell?" The drifter was mumbling, his voice still thick and slurred. "What's that smell? What's that smell?"

The man dumped the drifter to the floor and used his foot to roll him over the chalk line. He turned without a word and shut the door behind him. Then he leaned against the wall with his eyes closed until he heard the faint clink of chains. He did not allow himself to cover his ears. The drifter's voice was getting louder, clearer.

"Oh, God, Alice. Look at his eyes. Look at... What's that smell? What..."

The shriek was sudden and terrible. The drifter's screaming went on for far longer than the man would have liked, then ended in a long gargle and a wet slap. For a long time, there was only a soft grunting sound.

The man sat for a while, trying not to think. In the dark of the factory and the mostly quiet, he may have dozed. He could not tell.

Eventually the man got to his feet, retrieved his backpack and entered the office. He looked down at the little girl, chained to the wall, whose face was still angelic beneath the sheen of gore. Her cheeks were bulging out, and the man almost caught himself smiling. Old habits.

The drifter was...not. Not anymore. The man used his

crowbar to drag the pile of rag and bone into a corner and then turned back to the little girl. She looked at him with wide eyes, her face framed by fair, clean hair. She swallowed the mouthful of meat, and the man watched as the huge lump pushed down her throat and settled in a belly already swollen beyond reasonable capacity.

"Let's get you cleaned up," said the man.

He took care to stay on his side of the chalk line. A chain tethered the little girl from a collar around her neck to a ring set deep in the concrete of the office wall. She made no noise, but quietly strained against her bonds, her toes pushing against the white line. In a quick, practiced movement, the man placed a strip of electrical tape over the girl's mouth. She did not react. He taped her hands together, with the same ease of familiarity.

There was something of a ceremony, the man unpacking items of bright color onto a clean white towel. He stripped the girl of her simple blue nightshirt and began to wipe her down with wet-wipes, slowly accumulating a small mountain of pink used tissue. He changed her diaper, which was already filled with barely digested meat. He carefully and lovingly washed her hair, using the blue, bear-shaped bottle. There was a bandage on her left arm. He changed it, cleaning and sterilizing the wound underneath that he knew would never heal. After a time, she was dressed again. Her clean hair combed, the duct tape removed from her angelic face.

"Who do you want tonight?" said the man. He held up a couple of ragged stuffed animals. "Mister Bear or Captain Squirrel?"

The girl said nothing.

"Mister Bear, I think," said the man, sliding the cuddly toy carefully across the concrete. The girl did not break her gaze to look at the bear. Her eyes remained fixed on the man.

"Are you ready for a story?"

The girl said nothing.

The man opened a garishly colored and shiny covered book and turned to a neatly folded page. "Benny Bunny Goes to Market. It was a rainy Tuesday, and Benny Bunny was supposed to meet Danny Dog for a picnic, but he could not for the life of him find his umbrella..."

In the soft glow of the lamplight, the girl stood motionless while the man read on into the night. Eventually he stood and looked at her for some time. When he spoke, there was a quiet choke in his voice.

"I'm going to go to bed now, okay?"

The girl said nothing.

The man reached out unthinkingly to stroke an errant hair away from her eye. He moved his hand back just in time as her teeth snapped in a sudden feral snarl. He looked at her for a long while.

"Good night, princess. I love you."

That night the man wept, as he wept every night, biting hard on his hand to stop himself sobbing aloud. Through the broken factory windows, the low sounds of the city at night drifted, a low, mournful dirge of whispering voices. It was almost sympathetic, nearly merciful, when they called to him like that.

The next morning brought more of the same. More electrical tape, more cleaning. More stories and songs. More cleansing of dead meat from full diapers. The man ate his soup and, as always, offered some to the little girl, who, as always, looked past the spoon and at the man's fingers.

126

He did not bury what was left of the drifter. The bones were sucked clean by the time he had awoken that morning.

"Say something," he said. "Say 'daddy.' Say 'mommy.' Do you remember mommy?"

The girl said nothing. The man brought a folded photograph out of his pocket; it showed a woman holding a baby, eyes tired but mouth smiling. "Do you remember mommy? Can you say 'mommy'?"

The girl frowned for a moment, the first change in her expression that day. Her lips parted, and the man held his breath. The little girl moaned. Not a moan of sadness, or sickness. Just an empty noise of appetite and hunger. The same noise she always made, now.

"Oh, my little girl," he said.

He could not fathom his own sadness. Nor the urge to hold her. Those mental tools he needed to construct and delineate his feelings were lost a long time ago, and all he felt now was a wave of aching that seemed to crush him like a second gravity. He held out his hand and touched her hair. A small part of him hoped that she would look up with recognition in her eyes, that her memories of Christmases and Easters and bath times and bedtimes would prove stronger than her endless appetite. Part of him knew better.

The bite was quick and ragged, nearly severing his pinkie finger. The man nodded and stood up. Using his crowbar, he prodded the little girl in the chest, keeping her at bay as he made his way to the chains. He undid the padlock that held them in place and hurried from the room.

Later, he sat in a dark corner, hearing the moan of the little girl as she shuffled around the factory, looking for him. He wondered how long the gestation period was. It seemed to vary with blood group. His wife had been quick. The girl, slow. He found time to regret the drifter. But not much.

Outside the factory, the streets are crowded and quiet. Huge groups of shuffling figures pick their way slowly over crashed cars and scattered litter. Here and there lay the bones of those not quick enough or lucky enough, ragged and reaching across the crumbling tarmac, each the center of their own dark stain. Among the figures, a man walks in no particular direction, a little girl by his side. His hand dangles at his side, almost, but not quite, touching her hair.

a fistful of sugar

Well, this has all been a bit full on, hasn't it? A bit dour? A bit serious? Well, let's go out with a chuckle.

I was asked to contribute to the *Quick Draw!* anthology by Noah K. Sturdevant where the only requirement was that I wrote something funny, and I wrote it in a thousand words or less. I was really glad to get the offer. I was lucky enough to write short form internet comedy in its hay day (remember Cracked.com? When it was good, I mean?) and I'd almost forgotten how much fun it was to just be a silly goof for a page or so. I hope this one leaves you with a smile on your face.

a fistful of sugar

BUTLEIGH MANOR WAS a charismatic bundle of gray stone and iron wrought windows, nestled in ivy at the end of its long, graveled drive. On a good day you may have put it on a postcard.

On a good day.

But today was not a good day. Today the November winds blasted and rattled the windows, and a thick, gloomy sky belched thunder like an uncle who isn't quite drunk enough to be racist yet.

In the great hall, Lord Butleigh threw another log onto the fire, which is to say he stared pointedly at his man, Jenkins, until Jenkins put another log on the fire.

Britain at the turn of the century was a place of progress, and Lord Butleigh liked to consider himself a modern man. He'd only ever once punched a nanny, this year, at least, and he wasn't in a hurry to have Jenkins do it again. However, the nanny in question was being particularly annoying. Lord Butleigh adjusted his monocle and tried to focus on the sourdough face of his only son's nurse.

"I carn't take it any more me'lud, I simply carn't!" she wailed.

Butleigh blinked and looked over at Jenkins, who sighed. "She says she cannot bear any more of this endeavor, sire."

Butleigh harrumphed. It was a fine old harrumph, passed down through generations of Butleigh men. "Tell her it's what we bally well pay her for! A gentleman can't be expected to look after his own child. It's obscene!"

"But m'lud!" the nanny wept, crinkling her apron between her gnarled fingers. "The devil is in him, so it is. Right up his poor wee bottom hole, so it is."

Lord Butleigh looked at Jenkins, who shrugged. "Is this about the boy projectile vomiting on you?"

The nanny nodded meekly.

"And crawling around on the ceiling?"

The nanny nodded meekly.

"Gets it from his mother's side, you know." Lord Butleigh let his eyes drift upward to the portrait hanging over the hall's ludicrous stairway. His poor dead, awful wife looked down on him with the familiar empty gaze of someone who had never known an orgasm.

"Jenkins, throw this woman into the mud..." Butleigh remembered himself. "*Escort* this woman into the mud, and then put an advertisement into the local paper for a new nanny. One with a bit of experience in dealing with children that crawl around on the ceiling, and such."

Jenkins nodded and rolled up his sleeves. He froze as there was a booming knock at the door. The sound reverberated throughout the hall. The flames in the fireplace flickered.

Butleigh cleared his throat. "Well, don't just stand there, Jenkins. You can open the door and manhandle at the same time. Multi-task, damn you!"

Jenkins nodded and hoisted the struggling nanny above his head. In the practiced movement of a true professional, he wedged the door open with his foot, threw the shrieking old woman out into the dark, and then stepped smartly aside to welcome the new visitor.

Lord Butleigh felt his jaw go slack as a strange woman entered. Beautiful, but severe, dressed in an immaculate purple frock coat and pillbox hat. "Lord Butleigh, I presume?" she said, in a thankfully understandable dialect.

Butleigh nodded and the woman handed him a small white business card.

Ms. Mary Stabbins
"I will 'take care' of your children."

"What an astonishing coincidence," Butleigh gasped. "We were just as of this moment in the market for a new nanny."

"Astonishing," Mary agreed, flatly.

Jenkins cleared his throat. "Perhaps your lordship should explain that young master Butleigh is...somewhat of an unusual case?"

Mary Stabbins held up her neatly gloved hand. "Perhaps a demonstration of my capabilities before we negotiate my terms and salary?"

Butleigh raised his eyebrows. "Very well then," he concluded, and led the forthright young lady up the stairs and to his son's chambers. Inside the boy sat in the middle of the bed, dressed in his soiled nightdress. His eyes were two pupil-less eggs and his skin was a veiny, pallid green. He grinned terribly as his head slowly rotated.

Lord Butleigh made introductions. "Ms. Stabbins, this is my son, Farlington. As you can see, he has a touch of the demonic possessions."

"Eat a fuck ton of shit!" Farlington growled.

"Ah," said Mary. "Nothing I haven't seen before."

She approached the child, who fixed her with a demonic glare.

"Your mother sucks cocks in—"

The child was interrupted by a sudden cracking sound. His eyes went wider still, and he put a shaking hand to his cheek.

"Did you just slap me, wench? I'll—"

SLAP!

"Arrrgh! Ow!" the monster cried.

Butleigh beamed. "You seem to be getting through to him already!"

"Quite," said Mary. "Though it's best to be sure." From her skirts she pulled a long handle that Lord Butleigh first assumed was an umbrella, but then realized was a robust cane.

The demon boy gaped in horror. "Fuck this, I'm out!" he cried.

There was a tremendous fart from Farlington's nether regions. Butleigh swore he heard the shrieking of the damned as the boy seemed to deflate, his eyes turning back to their normal blue and his skin returning to the slightly less pallid shade of an English aristocrat.

"Whu... where am I?" He sniffed. "Daddy?"

SLAP!

"You will address your father as Lord Butleigh," Mary said.

"Well, I say!" said the Lord. "You seemed to have sorted the blighter out already!"

Mary nodded and patted the cane in her hand. "Quite so, Lord Butleigh, but if you don't mind, I'd like to finish the beating anyway. It tends to set an example."

"Why, of course!" Butleigh chuckled. "A good thrashing with a blunt instrument is excellent for building character. I'll leave you to it."

Lord Butleigh left the room and the helpless screams of his

son behind him. Along the stairs he stopped under the portrait of his wife and lingered a while. It was not an easy thing for a single father to raise a son by himself. He knew she would be proud of him.

about the author

Steve Wetherell the person is, for legal reasons, not affiliated in any way with the thoughts or actions of Steve Wetherell the author, who is, for the purposes of any official inquires, a fictional character. He is allegedly from the English Midlands, allegedly has children, and allegedly appears on the Authors & Dragons podcast. He likes beer and rock music and dislikes official inquiries. Allegedly.

also by steve wetherell

From Falstaff Books

The Last Volunteer

The Chained Immortal

The Mad Emperor

The Endless Adventures of Handen Strike

From Authors & Dragons

The Totally Legend of Brandon Thighmaster

Brandon Thighmaster and Some Other Guys (With EM Kaplan)

From the Shingles Series

The Monkey's Penis

Put Your Hand in My Ass

Space Werewolf from Planet Sex

I Know What You Dicked Last Summer

The Shingling

Silent But Deadly Hill

Unaffiliated

Shoot the Dead

Far into the Dark

A Dark Night Begins

www.ingramcontent.com/pod-product-compliance
Lightning Source LLC
Chambersburg PA
CBHW071249150726
48001CB00018B/469